## There's Something Evil in the Attic.

Jill Peterson didn't want to move to Fear Street. All her life, she heard the whispers. The rumors. The stories. About the terrible things that happen to people who live there.

And now they're all happening . . . to her.

It seems her new house is already occupied. You might even say haunted. By someone—or some*thing*—that can hurl heavy things through the air. Something that can make furniture come alive—and attack.

Something that wants Jill *out*.

D1167180

**Also from R. L. Stine**

The Beast
The Beast 2

*R. L. Stine's Ghosts of Fear Street*

Available from MINSTREL Books

For orders other than by individual consumers, Pocket Books grants a discount on the purchase of **10 or more** copies of single titles for special markets or premium use. For further details, please write to the Vice-President of Special Markets, Pocket Books, 1633 Broadway, New York, NY 10019-6785, 8th Floor.

For information on how individual consumers can place orders, please write to Mail Order Department, Simon & Schuster Inc., 200 Old Tappan Road, Old Tappan, NJ 07675.

# R·L·STINE'S
## GHOSTS OF FEAR STREET ®

# HOUSE OF A
# THOUSAND SCREAMS

A Parachute Press Book

A
MINSTREL ®
BOOK

PUBLISHED BY POCKET BOOKS

New York   London   Toronto   Sydney   Tokyo   Singapore

The sale of this book without its cover is unauthorized. If you purchased this book without a cover, you should be aware that it was reported to the publisher as "unsold and destroyed." Neither the author nor the publisher has received payment for the sale of this "stripped book."

This book is a work of fiction. Names, characters, places and incidents are products of the author's imagination or are used fictitiously. Any resemblance to actual events or locales or persons, living or dead, is entirely coincidental.

A MINSTREL PAPERBACK *Original*

 A Minstrel Book published by
POCKET BOOKS, a division of Simon & Schuster Inc.
1230 Avenue of the Americas, New York, NY 10020

Copyright © 1997 by Parachute Press, Inc.

*HOUSE OF A THOUSAND SCREAMS* WRITTEN BY
P. MacFEARSON

All rights reserved, including the right to reproduce this book or portions thereof in any form whatsoever. For information address Pocket Books, 1230 Avenue of the Americas, New York, NY 10020

ISBN: 0-671-00190-6

First Minstrel Books paperback printing February 1997

10  9  8  7  6  5  4  3  2  1

FEAR STREET is a registered trademark of Parachute Press, Inc.

A MINSTREL BOOK and colophon are registered trademarks of Simon & Schuster Inc.

Cover art by Mark Garro

Printed in the U.S.A.

**1**

"**S**omething bad is going to happen."

The voice came from right behind me. My hand jerked and knocked over the bottles I'd just arranged on my dresser. I spun around.

Of course, it was my little brother, Freddy.

"You twerp," I complained. "You should never sneak up on someone like that. Look! You made me spill talcum powder all over the dresser." I punched him in the shoulder, just hard enough to hurt a little.

"Ow!" He scowled. "What did you do that for, Jill?"

Actually, I felt sorry as soon as I did it. Freddy isn't bad as little brothers go. He's very serious. I sometimes call him the Brainiac. He's kind of a nerd, but he means well.

I would have apologized, but hey, I'm the older sister. Besides, he should have knocked.

"Scare me like that again and I'll *really* hit you," I told him. I turned and went back to unpacking. "Why are you in here anyway? You can't be done setting up your room already."

"Yes, I am," he said, hopping up on my bed. "Well, almost. But I started feeling . . . you know."

"What?" I asked him, grinning. "Nosy?"

Freddy didn't smile. "No—weird," he told me.

I didn't say so, but I knew what he meant. We had just moved to the one town we *never* thought we'd live in. A town our relatives always talk about in whispers. Shadyside. And we didn't *just* move to Shadyside. We moved to *Fear Street* itself.

It was all because of Uncle Solly. Well, great-uncle actually. Uncle Solly was our dad's mother's brother. When he died a few months ago, he left his house on Fear Street to Dad.

Dad always wanted to move back to Shadyside, where he grew up. And Mom always wanted a real house. So Dad arranged for his company to transfer him. And the Peterson family—that's us—picked up and moved. Just like that.

Freddy and I were nervous enough about moving. All our lives we'd lived in Texas. Shadyside was a big change. What would our new school be like? Would kids like us? Would they make fun of our accents?

And on top of all that, would we ever get used to living on Fear Street?

I remembered how the movers had acted that morning. I never saw guys move so fast in my life. You'd have thought all our boxes were on fire. It took them two hours to load the truck back in Texas. But once we got to Fear Street, they moved us in in twenty minutes flat.

Freddy's round face was serious. I sat beside him on the bed. "Look, dweeb, all that stuff about ghosts and monsters on Fear Street is just talk," I told him. "All families have stories like that. I'll bet lots of people have lived here on Fear Street for years and never seen anything weird."

"You think so?" He cocked his head and blinked at me from behind his glasses.

I had to laugh. With that round face, and his green eyes magnified by his thick lenses, my little brother looked exactly like an owl.

I, on the other hand, look more like a stork. I'm long and thin, with straight brown hair and brown eyes. Dad says I'll grow into my legs one day. I'm waiting.

"It isn't funny," Freddy complained. He sounded offended.

"Sorry," I said. I reached over and gave him a friendly noogie. "Don't forget, this was Uncle Solly's house. You loved him. He used to show you those magic tricks."

"Yeah, he was pretty neat." Freddy gazed down at his short legs swinging against the bed.

Uncle Solly had been a magician. Not just some guy who was interested in magic. Uncle Solly was *famous*. He traveled all over the world. He was a star! But to us he'd always been warm and kind. Even if he *was* a little strange.

Because of Uncle Solly, magic was Freddy's hobby. Uncle Solly always used to brag about how Freddy took after him. Uncle Solly even sponsored Freddy for membership in the International Brotherhood of Magicians.

Freddy grinned at me. "Remember, Mom always said he was too generous, and Uncle Solly would say—"

" 'You have to take care of the little people. Take care of the little people and you're set for life,' " I finished in a phony, deep voice. Freddy and I collapsed in giggles, remembering.

I leaned back on the bed. "The last time I saw him, he even brought it up again," I told Freddy. "Out of the clear blue, he said, 'Don't ever forget about the little people, Jill. Make friends with the little people, and you'll do okay.' I told him I was always nice to little kids. Then he got the strangest look and said, 'Oh, yeah. Them too.' "

"He was always joking," Freddy reminded me.

"Yeah, he was." I clapped Freddy on the back.

**4**

"Anyway, he lived here for years and years. And Uncle Solly wouldn't live someplace scary, would he?"

Freddy sat there and thought about it. I watched his face anxiously. I *had* to convince him. It was the first *real* house we'd ever lived in, and I could see how happy it made my mom.

Besides, the house really was great! It had two stories, and an attic, and extra bedrooms, and doors with old-fashioned key locks, and a big green lawn outside, and plenty of trees.

So what if there were other houses just a few doors down with cracking walls. So what if the street was lined with twisted trees that sometimes looked like monsters crouching over the sidewalk. That was someone else's problem.

"I guess you're right," Freddy finally admitted. He scratched the side of his head. "I *hope* you're right anyway." He turned and looked over my unpacked boxes. "Well, you better get busy. You have lots left to do."

I poked a finger in his chest. "I'd be done by now if you hadn't interrupted."

"Hah!" he scoffed. "If I hadn't come in, you'd be drooling over your poster of that guy from *Friends* by now."

I grabbed at him. He laughed and slid away.

"Oh, Joey!" he squealed in a girlie voice. "I love you!"

**5**

Grinning, I tackled him. We hit the floor rolling. "Take it back," I hollered. I grabbed his arm and pushed it up behind him. He was laughing so hard, he couldn't manage to pull away.

Then there was a crash. The floor shook. It sounded as if someone dropped a buffalo from the ceiling.

I let go of Freddy and we stared at each other in surprise. I glanced around the room. Nothing seemed to have moved.

"Did *we* do that?" Freddy asked.

Before I could answer, the room filled with noise. Thumps and bangs came from everywhere. First the wall in front. Then behind. I whipped my head back and forth, following the sounds.

"What is it?" I cried. "What's happening?"

Freddy pointed with a trembling hand. My eyes followed his finger. And then I stared.

I had a lamp made out of one of those pottery jugs, the kind you see in old Western movies. The lamp was big, heavy. And it was dancing and thumping on top of my dresser! The bottom clattered against the wood.

I jumped to my feet. "Earthquake!" I shouted.

"Oh, yeah?" Freddy said, his voice strangely high. "Then how come nothing else is moving?"

Before I could answer, the lamp snapped on and off. Then again. And again. The smell of burning wires stung my nose. I grabbed Freddy to shove him out of the room.

**6**

My bedroom door slammed shut. *By itself.*

The thumping noise suddenly stopped. We turned and put our backs to the door. The lamp rose from the dresser. Its cord whipped free of the socket.

The lamp shot across the room—and flew straight toward my head!

**F**reddy and I threw ourselves to the floor, screaming. The lamp exploded against the door behind us. Pieces of glass and pottery flew everywhere. We lay still for a moment, afraid to move.

Finally, I got to my feet. I shook bits of lamp from my hair.

"Whoa!" Freddy said. "That was close!"

I heard footsteps running up the stairs. My bedroom door swung open, nearly whacking me in the head. Mom stood in the doorway, her eyes wide at the sight of the crumpled lamp shade and pieces of lamp all over the floor.

"Look at this mess!" she cried. "What have I told you two about roughhousing?"

"Mom, we didn't do anything—" I began to explain.

"Oh, Jill. I heard you two wrestling around up here. Now look what you've done."

"But it's true, Mom," Freddy insisted. "We didn't do anything. There was just this loud noise and then—"

"—and then the lamp just got up and flew across the room all by itself, I suppose," Mom finished.

"Well . . . yeah." Freddy's cheeks turned red. We both realized how stupid that sounded.

Mom looked annoyed. "Honestly. I may have been born in the morning, but not *this* morning."

"But—" I protested.

"No buts, Jill," Mom said sternly. "I want you to get this stuff cleaned up. And part of what that lamp cost is coming out of your allowances."

"Aw, Mom," Freddy groaned. He looked at me for help.

I knew better than to argue any more. Mom would never believe us if we tried to tell her what happened. I wasn't sure I believed it *myself*. And I had watched it!

"We're sorry, Mom," was all I said. "We'll clean it up."

"That's better." We must have seemed pretty down, because Mom's face softened. She offered a smile. "I know you're excited. I'm excited too. All

**9**

those years of apartments and renting from other people." She reached out and touched a wall. "Now we finally have a real home. Isn't it wonderful?"

I followed Mom downstairs and got the broom and dustpan. Mom went back to mounting her special collector's plates on the den walls. Thank goodness it wasn't one of *those* that broke. Mom loves her collection.

I returned to my room. Freddy had already picked up the biggest pieces of the lamp, the shade, and a big chunk of the base. He took them to the garbage outside while I swept up the rest of the mess as best I could. I had to rip my yellow spread off my bed and shake it out the window. Bits of glass and pottery were everywhere.

Finally I was finished. Leaning the broom against the wall, I glanced at the door where the lamp had crashed into it.

Weird! I frowned and reached out to run my hands over the door. There was no mark from the lamp slamming into it. No dents. No scratches in the paint. Nothing.

"It's like nothing ever happened," I whispered to myself. How was that possible? My lamp must have weighed at least ten pounds. And it had slammed into that door *hard*. There should have been a big dent. In fact, there should have been a *hole!*

Maybe it was just a freak accident.

*Or maybe it's Fear Street!*

No. I shook my head, trying to push the idea away. I was going to give myself nightmares if I started thinking like that.

Time to finish setting up my room. I grabbed a rag and crossed to my dresser. The powder I'd spilled before was still there.

As I was reaching to wipe it up, I stopped short. What were those strange marks in the powder?

My heart gave a slow, hard *thump*. It didn't make sense, I knew. But those marks on the dresser top . . .

They looked like tiny little footprints!

# 3

I rubbed my eyes and looked again.

They were still there. Tiny little tracks.

There must have been a mouse in my room, I thought. Yes, that was it. I made a face. I wasn't happy about having a mouse for a roommate. But what else could have made tracks that size?

The mouse must have knocked over my lamp too. Of course! Everything was starting to make sense.

Then I peeked at the tracks again. A cold finger of doubt tickled at my mind. The little prints might be mouse-sized. But did mice really have human-shaped feet?

Or, rather, *almost* human. Only four toes on each print.

And now that I looked again, the tracks weren't *that* small.

I dug in a box and found an old Barbie doll. Not that I still play with Barbies. It's just that I never throw anything away. Mom says I'm a pack rat.

I compared the size of Barbie's feet to the tracks. The tracks on my dresser seemed a bit shorter and wider. But they were nearly the same size. Were mice feet that big? A mouse with feet the size of Barbie's would be a hefty mouse.

More like a rat!

Ugh!

Shuddering at the thought, I quickly wiped up the powder. Maybe when the lamp was thumping and bumping around it made those marks, I reasoned. It was simply a coincidence that they looked like tiny little human feet.

But even so, the question remained: What made the lamp dance like that?

I finished unpacking and put the cleaning stuff away. Whatever happened, there had to be a perfectly rational explanation. No way was I going to start off in our new house afraid of my own bedroom.

Besides, I *liked* my new bedroom. It was big and airy, with plenty of space to play board games or hang with friends.

Assuming, of course, I managed to make some friends.

My window had a big wide sill you could sit on.

Through the window I could glimpse the old mill, and the blue of the Cononona River behind it. This summer Freddy and I planned to find out if the fish in Shadyside were any easier to catch than the ones back home in Texas.

Sighing, I got up to go downstairs. I stopped in the hall and gazed past Mom and Dad's bedroom to the attic stairs.

I'd avoided the attic so far. Attics are creepy places. If we did have mice—or *rats*—that's where they'd live.

And if we didn't have mice or rats—if we had something else . . . *something worse* . . .

I shook my head, angry with myself. I had to stop thinking like that. Had to stop wondering if we'd have been better off staying in Texas. This was home now. Shadyside. Fear Street.

Just the same, I was staying *out* of that attic!

I went down to the den. Mom had finished mounting her plates. She had dozens of them. Each one was in a separate holder that kept it snug against the wall.

The room looked great now that it was all furnished. Across from Mom's plate display was a brick fireplace. Next to that we had put the entertainment center, with a big comfortable couch facing it. White bookshelves ran across the other two walls. More books sat in the middle of the fireplace mantel, special antique ones that Mom liked to show off.

Freddy was crouched by the fireplace, digging

through a cardboard box he'd dragged from the closet by the television.

He gave me an excited look. "Check these out. They're old movies of Uncle Solly's magic act."

I peered over his shoulder. Little tin canisters were piled in the box. Labels were taped to them. PARIS, 1968 one read. CAESAR'S PALACE, LAS VEGAS, 1969 said another.

"Too bad we don't have a movie projector," I remarked.

"Aha!" Freddy cried triumphantly. He rose with a videotape in his hand. "I guess Uncle Solly had a couple of them converted to video. Want to see?"

"Definitely," I agreed. We'd never seen Uncle Solly's act. Sure, he'd done lots of tricks for us. Close-up magic and sleight of hand—that sort of thing. But his stage act was where he did the big tricks. The really excellent ones.

I popped the video into the VCR while Freddy pushed the box back into the storage closet. The two of us plopped onto the couch and put our feet up on the coffee table.

"This must have been filmed a really long time ago," Freddy whispered as the tape began.

I nodded. Freddy had to be right. Uncle Solly looked much younger in the tape than Freddy and I had ever seen him. But he was still big and fat, and his cape flared behind him. He wore a pair of wire-rimmed glasses, perched on the very end of his nose.

Although the video was in color, there was no sound track. Uncle Solly's mouth moved, but you couldn't hear what he was saying.

Not that you needed to. Watching him was good enough. His hands blurred as they plucked cards and silk scarves and flowers from the air. His wand turned into a huge silk square. Then, from the empty square, he produced a live pig! I'd never seen a magician produce a *pig* before.

All the while, things floated around Uncle Solly. Tables, chairs, fishbowls, boxes—even a volunteer from the audience. How did they stay up? Freddy and I stared and stared, but we couldn't see any wires. Only good old Uncle Solly, calmly doing his card tricks and rope tricks.

Finally, he moved his hands as if he were twirling a lasso. We laughed as he jumped through an imaginary loop. Then he made sweeping motions with his arms, spinning the invisible lasso above his head. He turned to the side of the stage and cast his loop. It looked exactly as if he were roping a steer!

"Yee-hah!" Freddy yelled.

I stared, fascinated. Uncle Solly was hauling on his imaginary rope as if he'd lassoed a wild bull. From the stage wings floated a table with a box on top. We laughed at the way the table seemed to fight against the invisible rope. "How did he *do* that?" I cried.

Soon Uncle Solly brought the table under control.

It settled to the stage in front of him. The camera swept over the applauding audience and then back to a smiling, bowing Uncle Solly. We clapped too. "Someday I'm going to be as good as he was," Freddy vowed.

Uncle Solly's beaming smile seemed to fade a little as he turned back to the box. The camera zoomed in, and we could see the box clearly. Its front was decorated with ugly, grinning carved faces.

Uncle Solly's forehead creased, and his hands fluttered in the air over the box. "Wow! He looks like he's really concentrating," Freddy whispered.

"That's just part of the act," I answered.

The box lid suddenly flew open.

A big, hairy monster stuck its head out.

"Whoa!" Without thinking, I jerked back in my seat.

The monster was ugly. *Really* ugly. It opened its mouth and we gasped at the sight of dripping greenish fangs. Its long, clawed fingers tore at the rim of the box. Its blue fur looked greasy and matted. Its eyes held an evil red glare.

Uncle Solly flicked his fingers. The monster swayed, its gaze glued to Uncle Solly's magic hands.

"That's one ugly puppet," Freddy murmured.

So that's what it was. A puppet. I felt stupidly relieved. "How does it move?" I asked. "I don't see any strings."

Freddy rolled his eyes. "If you knew anything about magic, you'd know the puppeteer is underneath the table," he said in his most superior, Brainiac voice.

"Oh, yeah?" I retorted, annoyed. "Well, I'm looking under the table right now. And there's nothing there but table legs."

"It's a mirror trick," Freddy answered. As if that explained everything.

On the tape, Uncle Solly stopped waving his hands and stepped back.

The puppet began to move on its own! Balls and rings popped out of the air around it, and the puppet juggled them. First three. Then four. Then seven. Then nine!

"That's impossible," Freddy said.

I was still annoyed with him. "Obviously not," I replied.

Freddy shook his head vigorously. "No, it really is unbelievable!" he declared. "It looks like real magic! No puppeteer could do that—make a puppet juggle nine balls."

"Just because you don't know how it's done—"

I broke off in mid-sentence. What was that scraping sound? It came from somewhere near the fireplace.

At first I couldn't figure it out. Everything seemed normal. Then I noticed. The books on the mantelpiece were on the far right end. Hadn't they been in the middle?

I turned to my brother. "Freddy, I—" I started to say.

*Swish!*

I glanced back at the mantelpiece. My heart beat faster. Now the books were on the far *left* end.

Freddy was so absorbed in the magic show, he didn't notice. Keeping my eyes on the books, I reached out to shake him. Just as I touched his shoulder, the books zipped to the other end.

*Swish!*

Fear rippled through me. "Freddy," I whimpered. "It's happening again."

The books began to move without stopping, back and forth across the mantel. *Swish—swish—swish!*

Freddy leaned forward, peering at the TV screen. "Wow, the puppet is eating all that junk it was juggling."

"Would you forget the video?" I squeaked. "Look at this."

He glanced at the moving books. They were picking up speed. Out of the corner of my eye I saw his mouth fall open.

All at once the books stopped, dead center, on the mantel. We sat like stone, afraid to move.

"Is it over?" Freddy whispered.

Something made me look at the tall white bookshelves. They stood on opposite sides of the room. With us in the middle.

The books on those shelves were jostling up and

19

down. Their covers rubbed against each other, making a noise like a crowd of people whispering.

"I don't think so," I said in a low voice.

The movement on the white shelves increased. Dozens of books danced in place, faster and faster. Now they sounded like angry, whirring insects.

I was so scared, I couldn't move. This wasn't possible. It couldn't be happening. Why were the books shaking like that? What would happen next?

Then I had a horrible thought.

"Freddy?" I whispered. "Remember the lamp?"

"Yeah." His voice was tense. "So?"

On his last word the books leapt from the shelves on either side. They flew through the air, hurtling toward us!

"So *duck!*" I yelled, and hit the floor.

# 4

Freddy followed me in a flash. And just in time too!

Books shot from either side of the room. They slammed together in the air above our heads. Heavy volumes fell all over us. "Ow!" I heard Freddy muttering. "Ow! *Ow!*"

Then the rain of books ended almost as quickly as it began.

I lifted my head cautiously and peeped around the room. Everything normal. Above me I heard a door slam and the sharp stride of Mom's shoes in the upstairs hall.

"Oh, no," I groaned. Books littered the room. It was a total wreck. How could this happen twice in one day?

Freddy stood and brushed himself off. "On the bright side, at least nothing broke this time."

At that, one of Mom's special collector's plates tumbled from the wall rack.

I barely managed to leap and catch it before it hit the floor. I was stretched out like a baseball player, Mom's beloved Elvis in Hawaii plate in my hand, when she walked through the door.

Her eyes widened in horror. Her head swiveled slowly, taking it all in. When she got to me, she simply stopped and stared.

"Hi, Mom," I said with a weak grin.

On the videotape the monster puppet and Uncle Solly were silently juggling books, tossing them back and forth across the stage. Mom sighed.

"Don't you know it takes years of practice to juggle like that?" she said. Bending down, she took the plate from my hand. She returned it to its rack on the wall. "And you certainly don't practice in the den, where you might break my precious Elvis plate. Among other things."

I rose slowly and glared at the video. Of course, I knew it was ridiculous. But it almost seemed as if the whole thing had been planned. Planned to make Freddy and me look bad.

Mom picked up a couple of the books. "And another thing. Start with two or three objects apiece. Don't just stand across from each other, chucking all the books in the shelves." She held one up. "Look. The spine on this is ruined." She glanced at Freddy.

"I'm especially disappointed in you, Freddy. I thought you had more respect for books."

"Sorry," he said in a small voice.

I could tell by the glare he gave me that he wanted to tell Mom the truth. But I just shook my head. What good would it do? It was our bad luck that it all happened just when the video got to the part about book juggling.

Mom went to the door, then turned to face us. "You two clean this mess up and try—*try*—to see if you can make it to dinner without destroying any more property."

"Got it," I answered, feeling glum.

Mom left and we started cleaning up. After a few minutes Freddy said, "We should tell her."

"What's the point? She won't believe us," I argued. "Especially after seeing that act on the tape."

"Well, then, we'll find a way to *make* her believe us!" Freddy's eyes were scared. "Some of these books are heavy. We could have really been hurt, Jill."

"But we weren't," I pointed out. "We don't know what happened, Freddy. Maybe the books just fell out of the shelves."

"Yeah, right. Books don't fall fifteen feet across a room, stupid."

I picked up another armload of books. "How do you know there's not a natural cause? Maybe Shadyside is on some kind of what-do-you-call-it—fault line. Maybe it was an earthquake."

"And maybe it's because we're on Fear Street," Freddy retorted.

This was getting ridiculous. "Look, Freddy," I said in my most reasonable voice. "You already expected something scary to happen. You said it yourself this morning. Remember?"

He nodded reluctantly.

"See? That's all it is," I told him. "We're both nervous and we've made this whole thing into too big a deal."

Freddy can be stubborn sometimes. "Maybe. But I still think we should tell," he insisted.

"Come on!" I shoved the last book back into place and faced him. "Can you just picture us telling Mom and Dad about how the books started dancing? Or how they flew off the shelves and tried to bean us? Think about it, Freddy. We'd either get grounded for lying or sent to the loony bin."

"Okay, okay!" Freddy scowled at me. "We won't say anything. But you better be right about those natural causes, Jill."

"I am," I assured him.

He left the den and clattered up to his room. I stared at the bookshelves. I wished I felt as sure of myself as I had sounded. Maybe we did live on a fault line. Or maybe there was some other natural explanation I hadn't thought of.

Or maybe we were in big trouble.

# 5

My first day at Shadyside Middle School went like a dream. A *bad* dream. By lunch period I was ready to go home and stay there. Maybe forever.

I stood at my locker, trying to ignore the stares and whispers of kids around me. I just *knew* they were talking about me. I'd heard them snickering in first period when I spoke. Everybody thought my Texas twang was funny. Now I was afraid to say anything.

It wasn't that I'd never been the new kid before. I had. But at least that had still been in Texas. At Shadyside I wasn't just new. I was different. I talked different. My clothes were different.

"Hi," a voice said behind me. I felt myself stiffen. *Oh, no, here it comes,* I thought. I grabbed my history book, closed my locker, and turned to face the music.

"Hi." I spoke quietly, prepared for teasing.

A blond girl stood watching me, her books held close to her chest. She gave me a friendly smile. "Nervous, huh? I know the feeling. I was new last year. I'm Breanna."

Shyly, I held out my hand to shake. "I'm Jill. Glad to meet you."

"Wow, you're so formal!" Breanna giggled. But she did shift her books so she could shake.

"Hey, Breanna. Checking out the new kid?" A boy walked up, smiling. He had longish hair, parted in the middle, and big brown eyes, like a puppy's. He held out his hand to me. "So nice to meet you. Charmed. I'm Bruce Codwallop the Third. Do you have a business card?"

I shook my head, confused. He pumped my hand. Then a laugh exploded out of him.

My cheeks started to burn. "I don't get the joke," I admitted.

Breanna was laughing too. "Sorry. It's just that we don't shake hands much here. Except with grown-ups, I mean."

I wanted to jump in my locker and close the door. "I'm sorry, I didn't know—"

"Don't worry," Breanna told me. "It's kind of nice. Bobby shouldn't have teased you."

I frowned. "Bobby?"

The boy grinned at me and asked Breanna, "Did

you tell her all the news yet? How I'm class president, and captain of the football team—"

"In your dreams!" Breanna tossed her head and turned back to me. "Ignore him. He thinks he's funny."

"I *am* funny," the boy shot back. "Breanna's just jealous. I'm in your class actually. My name's really Bobby Taylor."

"Oh, I see. Too bad. I thought Bruce Codwallop suited you better," I said coolly.

"Scorched!" Breanna declared. She leaned against Bobby and shoved him with her shoulder.

They looked a lot alike, I noticed. "Are you guys related?" I asked.

Breanna nodded. "He's my dorky twin."

Bobby grinned at me. "We share everything but looks and talent. I got all of them. That's why she gets the big bedroom at home. Mom and Dad feel sorry for her."

"So, do you think you're going to like it here?" Breanna asked.

"It's all so new." I shrugged. "I hope so."

"How do you like Mr. Gerard?" Bobby demanded.

I felt nervous. Actually, the math teacher gave me the willies, but what if everyone else liked him? I finally offered, "I can't tell yet. Why? Is there something wrong with him?"

"I think he's creepy," Breanna whispered.

**27**

"I heard he had a computer chip implanted in his head so he could solve equations faster," Bobby said. "The guy's very weird."

Breanna leaned against the locker next to mine. "Ms. Munson teaches art. She's nice, but strict."

"Likes to give new kids detention," Bobby put in.

"Shut up, Bobby," Breanna ordered. Glancing around, she leaned forward. "But then there's Mrs. McCord for science."

"What's wrong with her?" I asked.

Bobby said in a low, dramatic voice, "She's *mean.* Maybe even a little psycho. She really enjoys dissecting frogs, if you know what I mean. She giggles when she cuts them open, and her eyes sort of shine—"

"Yeah, right," I scoffed. I was trying not to let Bobby creep me out.

"And she likes to pop their legs into her mouth," he added. "Raw. Slurp!"

I stared at him. I couldn't think of anything smart to say. Instead, I blurted out, "Wow, you're gross!"

"He's not lying," Breanna assured me. "Well, maybe about eating the frogs . . . but she does seem to get a kick out of killing them."

My shoulders slumped. Great. A psycho science teacher! "Science is already my worst subject," I groaned.

"Never mind. You'll be fine. Come on, I'll show you around." Breanna raised her eyebrows at Bobby. "Don't you have somewhere to go?"

Bobby waved at me and sauntered off, popping the lockers with his knuckles as he went by.

Breanna took me to the lunchroom and introduced me to a couple of her friends. That was a huge relief. I'd been dreading lunch more than anything.

The rest of the day went better, though I still noticed kids whispering and pointing my way. I hated it. I hated feeling different. But at least I'd made a friend. I hoped.

I was thinking about that when I walked into my science class. I was early, since I didn't see Breanna, and I didn't know anyone else to hang around and be late with.

I walked in and saw a woman bent over a lab table. She was staring down at something green. It was a frog, I realized.

She reached down. Picked up the frog. Held it close to her face as if she were inspecting it.

And then she stuffed the whole thing into her mouth!

My books fell out of my hands and thudded to the floor. I screamed.

The woman whirled. The frog's legs dangled from her mouth.

And they were twitching!

The woman gazed at me, wild-eyed. Then—

*Slurp!*

She sucked the rest of the frog into her mouth!

# 6

**"O**h, *gross!*" I blurted out. I thought I was going to throw up. I spun and raced for the door.

Then I saw the crowd of kids in the doorway. They were all howling with laughter. Breanna and Bobby were among them.

I stopped cold. It was all a joke!

Still shaking, I turned. The teacher was pulling a rubber frog from her mouth. She winked at me.

"I'm the 'evil' Mrs. McCord. Hello, Jill, and welcome to Shadyside." She held the frog in front of her face. "Looks real, doesn't it?"

Kids were filing into the room, taking their desks, still laughing over the joke. Bobby clapped me on the back.

"Sorry," he said. "We couldn't resist. Mrs. McCord

is the coolest teacher in Shadyside. She loves practical jokes."

"And they happen to be a Taylor family specialty," Breanna chimed in. She looked at me with anxious brown eyes. "You aren't mad, are you?"

I managed to give her a grin. I *was* a little angry, but I knew better than to show it. Nobody likes a sorehead.

"Someday, somehow, I'm going to get y'all for this," I said out loud.

Mrs. McCord heard me. "Gosh, I hope so," she said. "Life's no fun unless you've got a nice, juicy revenge to look forward to." She directed me to a seat. "I think you're going to fit in just fine, Jill," she added with a smile.

Class settled down quickly after that. And I had to admit, Mrs. McCord really was a good teacher. Class was fun and lively, but she never let us stray too far from the subject. I'd always hated science before. But now I found myself drawn in. The way she explained things, it all made sense.

When the bell rang, I threaded my way through clumps of chattering kids to my locker. I made sure I had what I needed for homework, and went outside to find Freddy. The elementary school let out earlier than Shadyside Middle School, but I knew he would be waiting for me. He'd want to tell me about *his* first day.

Sure enough, he was there, sitting on the curb. I called to him and he fell into step beside me.

"Well, how did it go?" I asked.

Freddy hitched up his glasses. His face was glum. "A couple of kids picked on me. I'll probably have to fight somebody one of these days," he announced.

"You know what Mom says about that," I warned. "Look. If one of those little jerks gets out of hand, let me know. I'll take care of it for you."

He frowned. "No thanks. It's bad enough being new without hiding behind my sister!"

We crossed Park Drive, and took a right on Melinda toward Fear Street and home.

I couldn't believe how the neighborhood changed once you got to Fear Street. It was as if someone had drawn a line there and put up a big sign: BEWARE, ALL YE WHO ENTER HERE.

The trees that lined the sidewalk were twisted and knotty. And even though spring had arrived everywhere else in Shadyside, it didn't seem to have reached Fear Street yet. There were no new leaves, no crocuses. Bare brown tree branches tossed and rattled in the wind. It was spooky.

I felt better after we got through our own front door. I closed my eyes and breathed in the friendly smells. Maybe someday I'd get used to Fear Street.

In about a million years.

Mom was out shopping for dinner. She'd left us a note.

*Snacks are in the fridge. You can each have* one *cupcake and a piece of fruit. Back by four. Mom.*

At the bottom of the note was a P.S.

*Jill, I thought you liked your room the way it was. Why did you change it?*

"Huh?" I said, confused.

"What?" Freddy asked through a mouthful of cupcake.

I showed him the note. "I didn't change anything. What's she talking about?"

Freddy and I stared at each other. After a moment Freddy said, "Maybe we should find out."

We headed up to my room together. I stood at the door, my hand on the knob. My heart was pounding. It wasn't from climbing the stairs.

"Aren't you going in?" Freddy prodded me with his elbow.

"I'm going." I gritted my teeth and opened the door.

I gasped. *Everything* in my room had been moved! The bed now stood against the opposite wall. The dresser, so heavy that I couldn't budge it myself, was across the room from where it had been. My posters were all switched around.

"I didn't do this, Freddy," I said.

My little brother folded his arms. "So I guess it all just slipped out of place, like the books?"

**33**

He *would* pick that moment to go all superior on me.

I glared at him. "Don't get smart," I warned.

"Or maybe we have mice," he suggested sarcastically.

"That's enough. Cut it out!" I sat on the bed, got up again, and looked under it, just to make sure nothing was hiding there, then sat on the bed again. "What in the world could have done this?"

Freddy took a seat beside me. "I think I know," he told me. "But you're going to think I'm crazy."

"Look around you!" I waved my hand around my reorganized room. "Don't you think all *this* is crazy? I promise I won't laugh, Freddy. Just tell me your idea."

Freddy gnawed his lower lip for a moment, making up his mind. Then he jumped to his feet. "Wait here," he ordered and ran downstairs.

He came back up a moment later with a thick book. "I got this from my school library," he explained.

I took it from him and read the title aloud: *"Bumps in the Night: Real Stories of Hauntings in America."*

My hands shook. I licked my lips.

"You mean . . ." I trailed off. I couldn't say it.

Freddy could. He nodded.

"Yup," he said. "I think this house is haunted."

# 7

"**H**aunted!" I echoed. My hands suddenly felt clammy.

"Yeah! Everything fits, Jill," Freddy told me earnestly. He pointed to the book. "I think we've got a poltergeist."

"A poltergeist?" I repeated. I was starting to feel like a parrot. "What's that?"

Freddy hopped onto the bed beside me. "It's a kind of spirit. Like a ghost. But its specialty is throwing things around."

I opened the book and Freddy showed me the section about poltergeists. The stories were a lot like ours. Things flying through the air, loud noises, stuff changed and rearranged.

"Look, Freddy," I gasped. "It says this one family

lost their house because of a poltergeist. It ran them off!"

"That's not the worst. In one house the father disappeared. His kids could hear him in the walls, but they never saw him again!" Freddy pushed his glasses up his nose. His eyes were wide. "What if that happened to Dad? Or to us?"

I decided there was no point thinking about *that*. "How do you get rid of them?" I asked. "Do you call a ghostbuster or something?"

Freddy shook his head. "I don't know. In most of those stories, it seems like the people just give up and leave. Or go crazy."

"Or disappear," I whispered. My mouth went dry. I felt a strange, tingly fear at the base of my spine. "What are we going to do?"

"Move," Freddy declared.

"We can't. It would break Mom's heart! Anyway, how could we possibly convince Mom and Dad to leave this house?"

"I keep telling you. We have to talk to them! We need to tell them the truth about what's been going on," Freddy insisted. "Do you really think they'll want to live in a house that has a poltergeist?"

"Do you really think they'll believe us?" I shot back. "Freddy, haven't you noticed that none of this stuff ever happens in front of them? Would *you* believe it if you hadn't seen it with your own eyes?"

Freddy's forehead wrinkled as he thought. "You're right," he said slowly. "I wonder why? Maybe the poltergeist is trying to make us look bad. Maybe it wants to get us in trouble."

That made me *mad*. I felt my hands curl into fists. "There has to be a way to get rid of this thing," I muttered. "And whatever that way is, we're going to find it."

"Right!" Freddy agreed.

Then we both sat there on my bed, staring at the walls. I knew Freddy was thinking the same thing I was.

We talked tough. But, really, we didn't have a clue how to get rid of a poltergeist!

After a moment I stood up. "We can't just sit around here spooked. We need to do something. Anything."

"Let's do something for Mom," said Freddy. "She's been pretty annoyed with us lately. Let's surprise her."

"You want to? What should we do?"

"Let's bake her a pie," Freddy suggested. "You make great pies."

I laughed. Freddy was the original pie eater. "Bake *Mom* a pie, huh?"

Freddy grinned at me. "Yeah. Cherry."

"Which just happens to be your favorite flavor."

Freddy made an innocent face. "It's for Mom. Nothing's too good for Mom."

"All right," I agreed. "But let's do it now, before she gets home and tells us no."

We ran downstairs, taking three steps at a time.

"What should I set the oven for?" Freddy called as he ran ahead.

"Three-fifty. But not so fast, bonehead. Let's make sure we have cherry pie filling first."

Freddy rifled the pantry while I took out a big mixing bowl.

"Ta-da!" He hurried over with two cans of cherry filling.

"Okay. You open them while I start the crust."

"We're making two, right?" Freddy demanded, licking his lips.

I shook my head, smiling. What a pig! "Yeah, sure. We're making two."

While Freddy opened the cans, I measured and sifted the flour. I'd been baking since I was eight years old. Dad claimed I made the best pie crust in the country.

We laughed and joked as we worked. Freddy brought me a measuring cup of ice water for the crust. I moved the big plastic flour canister over to make room for rolling the pie dough. Then I sprinkled flour across the countertop.

I was reaching into the canister for a little more, when I heard a bang behind me. I turned, just in time to see all our baking pans falling out of the cupboard.

"Ow! Ouch!" Freddy hollered. Baking sheets bounced off his head.

"Clutz," I called.

"I didn't do it!" he protested. "They just came out!"

My hand was still in the flour container.

Then something grabbed it. Something in the flour itself!

Something that held my wrist in a grip of iron!

# 8

I screamed. I couldn't help it—it just burst out of me.

Frantic, I pulled against the thing in the canister. But it held on to my hand like a vise. Whatever it was, it had cold claws. I could feel them.

My heart hammered in my chest. "Let me go!" I yelled.

Every drawer in the kitchen flew open. Knives, forks, and spoons jangled out of their plastic holders. The mixing bowl flipped over and shattered on the floor.

"Freddy! Help!" I called frantically.

But my little brother had his own problems. He dodged a rain of flying plates. Then he slipped in a puddle of cherry pie filling and landed facedown in it.

Whatever held me squeezed my wrist. Hard. I cried

out in pain. Then I put everything I had into one big tug.

The grip suddenly released. The canister leapt off the counter and banged into my forehead.

"Ow," I groaned. I fell back in a thick cloud of flour. It covered me, clotting my mouth and nose.

"Look out!" Freddy shouted from where he lay sprawled.

I glanced up. The measuring cup floated in midair above me. As I stared at it, it tipped. Ice water poured out.

"Aaahh!" I yelled. Icy trickles ran over my face and into my ears. The water mixed with the flour and turned my hair into a sticky, doughy mess. As soon as it was empty, the measuring cup dropped to the floor. Its job was done.

I clambered slowly to my feet. The kitchen was buried beneath a blanket of flour. It looked as if it had been bombed. Which was roughly how I felt.

"Freddy?" I groaned, then coughed out a chunk of dough. I tried again. "Freddy? Are you all right?"

His voice was so calm that I could tell he was really scared. "I've been better."

"Oh, *no!*" a voice exclaimed behind me.

I whirled to see Mom standing in the kitchen doorway. She held bags of groceries in both arms. Her mouth hung open in shock.

There was no sound, no movement while she took it

all in. The broken plates and bowls. The spilled silverware. The thick coat of flour everywhere.

Slowly, Mom set the grocery bags down on the floor. At last she looked at me, and her face kind of twisted up.

I tried to grin. My lips stuck together a little where the dough and water had made a paste.

"We—uh, we thought we'd bake you a pie," was the best I could manage.

"A pie," Mom repeated.

"Cherry," Freddy piped up from his place on the floor. He scraped some filling off the floor with his finger to show Mom.

Mom stood there, dazed, for another moment. Then she took a deep breath. "Your father will be home this evening," she said. "I'll let him talk to you about this. Yes, that's what I'll do. Some other time, maybe, *I'll* talk to you about it. In a month or so. When I've calmed down . . ."

Her words trailed off. She turned and sort of hobbled away.

"We'll clean it up," I yelled. But if Mom heard me, she gave no sign.

Slowly, silently, we started putting things right. Only four dishes had broken, thank goodness. And the mixing bowl.

The more I worked, the madder I got. What did the poltergeist have against *us* anyway? What had we ever done to it?

"Jill?" Freddy asked.

"Yeah?" I snapped.

Freddy's voice was small. "What do we do now?"

"Now?" I began sweeping the flour into a pile. "Now we finish making the kitchen as good as new."

"I meant after that," Freddy said.

I knew what he meant. But part of me couldn't believe what I was about to say. I took a deep breath. "All right. After that we find out where this poltergeist thing is hiding. Then we figure out a way to fix its little wagon."

"Are you serious?" Freddy squeaked. "Jill, poltergeists are supernatural. They have powers."

Poor Freddy! He looked so scared that I forgot my own fear. I had to make him feel better.

"So what?" I demanded. "We have powers too!"

"We do?" Freddy looked doubtful. "Like what?"

"Well . . ." I thought fast. "Uh—we're from Texas. It's like they say back home. Don't mess with Texas!"

Freddy was staring at me as if I had sprouted an extra nose.

I hurried on. "Texans are the roughest, toughest, smartest people around. Right?"

"If you say so," Freddy answered, still staring at me.

But I was starting to get into it. "You bet I do. Remember the Alamo!" I called, and punched my fist into the air.

"We lost at the Alamo," Freddy reminded me.

Oh, yeah, I thought. Well . . .

"It doesn't matter," I argued. "It's the Alamo spirit that matters. The Texas spirit. Where everything is bigger and better." I was really worked up by now. "What state's bigger than Texas?"

"Alaska."

I shook my head. Freddy wasn't catching my drift. "Alaska doesn't count."

"In fact," Freddy went on as if I hadn't spoken, "if you cut Alaska in half and made it two states, Texas would be the *third* biggest state."

"You are getting to be a major drag," I told him. "The point is, we're not quitters. Would Sam Houston quit?"

"No. He wouldn't."

"Would Davy Crockett quit? Would Jim Bowie quit?"

"They weren't Texans," Freddy objected.

"Okay, forget about them." I leaned forward. Time to pull out the big guns. *"Would the Dallas Cowboys quit?"*

Freddy's face lit up.

"The Dallas Cowboys! No way! They would never quit."

"And neither will we!" I grinned at my little brother. "Now, come on. We have a lot left to do before we can go hunting for that poltergeist."

We tore into the mess with a new spirit. As we cleaned, I thought about our plan of attack.

If a poltergeist was hiding out in the house, there

**44**

was only one place it could be. The one place Mom hadn't gotten around to organizing yet. The one place I'd carefully avoided ever since we moved in.

The spookiest, scariest room in the house.

The attic.

But were we brave enough to go up there?

# 9

**B**efore we did anything, I took a shower. I had to wash all the flour paste out of my hair. It wasn't easy.

Then Freddy and I tiptoed past Mom and Dad's room, where Mom lay, "resting."

"Shhh," I warned.

We climbed the narrow stairs and stopped at the attic door. Freddy whispered, "What do we do if we find it?"

"I don't know," I admitted. "But we have to do *something*. Maybe we could chase it out a window."

"Or spray it with bug spray," Freddy suggested.

I nodded. "Whatever it takes. I just can't handle another day like today."

My hair was still wet from the shower. Water dripped down my neck. It reminded me of the disaster in the kitchen. That made me mad all over again. I set my jaw and turned the knob.

Thick, musty air greeted us as we stepped into the attic. The shutters had slats that sifted the late afternoon sunlight. Tiger stripes of light and shadow lay over mysterious mounds of stuff.

I stepped forward quickly and pulled the string for the light. A bare bulb flickered on.

It wasn't so creepy with the extra light. The room was cluttered with Uncle Solly's old junk. Boxes lay everywhere. A rocking chair with a broken rail leaned in one corner, more boxes piled on its seat. A dress dummy draped in rotting fabric stood beside it. That must have belonged to Uncle Solly's wife, I guessed. She died years ago, before I was born.

"I don't see any poltergeist," Freddy said. "Do you?"

"No," I admitted. Now that we were there, I felt kind of stupid. What had I expected? That the thing would be sitting at a table playing solitaire?

Freddy ran a finger along one of the old boxes. "Wow. Uncle Solly sure had a lot of stuff, huh?"

"Yeah," I agreed. "And look at the dust and cobwebs. Nobody's been up here for a long time."

Freddy shifted a box from the top of a stack. He opened the top and looked in.

"Hey, look at this." He held up a book. "It's all about coin magic. And here's a book by Houdini! Cool! It's like a library of magic."

Freddy loves magic books. He doesn't have too many of his own because they're really expensive. So this box was like a treasure chest to him.

"This is great!" he said, beaming.

*We could be here for a while,* I thought. I opened another box. Inside were hundreds of fancy silk scarves. Some were plain. Others had designs that looked like magical symbols.

We found other things. Boxes filled with plastic thumbs and fingers. Hollow tubes with other tubes hidden inside them. Hats with secret compartments for storing rabbits. Old-fashioned ladies' bonnets— for what, I couldn't even guess. Also, Freddy got really excited over something he called an egg bag. I don't know. It just looked like an ordinary bag to me.

The attic was like a magician's museum. The more stuff we took down, the more stuff we found.

That's how we found the big tricks, the illusions. There was a kind of brace that Freddy said was used for making people look as if they were floating. He showed me how it worked. But there were some tricks that even he couldn't figure out.

"It's like I said before," Freddy told me. "I think some of Uncle Solly's act was real magic. That's why we can't make it work."

"Don't be dumb," I said. "That's impossible."

"Hah!" Freddy poked me in the side. *"I'm* not the one who wanted to come up here and search for a poltergeist."

At last we found an old trunk buried under piles of boxes. We dragged it into the clear. Freddy lifted the lid. Inside was a bunch of old magazines. And a wooden box carved with ugly, grinning faces.

"Hey! That's the puppet box we saw in Uncle Solly's video," I exclaimed.

I pulled the box from the trunk. It was about a foot long on each side, a perfect cube. And heavy for its size. I shook it. Something thumped inside.

The box had a broken latch at the top. A piece of wire was twisted through it to keep it closed.

"Open it," Freddy suggested.

I started to untwist the wire. I'd almost gotten it off, when I heard a scraping noise behind me. And then a squeak.

"What was that?" Freddy whispered. "A rat?"

"A *rat!*" The hair rose on the back of my neck. I thought of the tiny footprints I'd found on my dresser top. I didn't want to turn around. What if the rat was right behind me?

Just then the puppet box jerked in my hands. "Hey!" I cried.

"Jill. Look!" Freddy gasped.

I whipped around.

There *was* something right behind me.

But it wasn't a rat.

It was much, much worse!

# 10

I stared at the nightmare thing in front of me. My mouth opened and closed. But I couldn't manage to get my voice going.

The dressmaker's dummy! Somehow, it had come to life! It floated in the air. Drapes of rotting fabric spread from its form like bat wings. One of the ladies' bonnets floated above. Between the bonnet and the dress dummy, where a face should have been, there was—nothing. Just dark, empty space.

Then the dummy swooped down at me!

"Look out!" Freddy screamed.

I yelped and stumbled backward. The fabric shaped itself into tattered hands and wrapped around the box I was holding. It tried to pull the box from my hands!

I hung on, too scared to let go. I wanted to scream. But I couldn't breathe.

Freddy hammered at the dummy with his fists. "Leave my sister alone!" he yelled.

I made a last desperate pull to get away. The box slid out of my sweaty hands and I fell backward.

But the dress dummy's fabric hands couldn't hold on either. The box hit the floor with a clatter. The top sprang open. I heard a *whoosh* of air.

Above me, the lightbulb exploded in a shower of glass.

And then everything went quiet again.

The dress dummy stood by the chair, where it belonged. The fabric was just fabric. The bonnet lay on the floor.

I sat there, dazed. And scared.

And mad.

If the poltergeist was trying to scare us away, its little plan had just backfired. Big time.

No poltergeist was going to drive *me* out of our new house!

Freddy ran to me. "Are you all right?"

"I'll live. Thanks for trying to rescue me." I grabbed his arm and pulled myself to my feet.

"Maybe we should get out of here, huh?" he asked hopefully.

"Wait a minute," I said. "We came up to find a poltergeist, right? Well, it's definitely here."

"Right. We found it. So let's go, okay?" Freddy started toward the door.

"Would you hold on?" I demanded, grabbing his arm. "We have to figure out how to fight it. Maybe there's something up here that will show us how. Let's look around a little more, okay?"

Freddy swallowed. "Okay," he agreed.

As he stepped toward me, his foot hit the box that the dummy and I fought over. Something small and shiny slid out and skidded a few inches along the floor.

"Hey." Freddy bent down and picked up a pair of glasses. "These were in the box." He handed them to me, then picked up the box. "Nothing else. The puppet isn't in here. Uncle Solly must have stuck him somewhere else."

I examined the spectacles. They were old-fashioned. Wire rims framed narrow rectangular lenses. The lenses were super thick, like Coke-bottle bottoms.

I put them on.

I don't need glasses, so these should have made everything blurry for me. But I could see perfectly clearly.

I pulled them off again and studied them. They *looked* like ordinary thick glasses.

I slipped them on again. Nothing.

"They're just plain glass," I said, surprised.

I handed them to Freddy. He took off his own and

slipped them on. "You're nuts. These are exactly the same prescription as my glasses!"

"No way!" I protested. Freddy has a heavy-duty prescription. Without his glasses he's pretty much a mole person—totally blind.

I took the glasses from him and tried them on again. They were clear as a windowpane. I could see perfectly.

How could they work for me *and* for Freddy?

There was something very strange about these glasses.

Something moved at the edge of my vision. My heart thumped. I jerked my head around.

Nothing there.

Squinting, I studied the shadows along the wall.

"What's up?" Freddy whispered.

I held up my hand to keep him quiet. *There.* A shadow moved behind one of the boxes. I was sure of it.

"There's something there," I whispered. "I can almost see it."

Slowly, I moved sideways to get a better look.

And there he was.

He looked like a tiny man, but covered all over with woolly brown hair. He stood on little bow legs, like a hairy cowboy. He couldn't be more than six inches tall. His lips poked forward, pooching out into a tube, kind of like a straw. Little black eyes glinted above a flat nose.

I felt a shiver of fear. Was this the poltergeist?

The hairy little man raised a hand and scratched his face. I saw the long, sharp nails on his hand. I remembered the claws of the thing in the flour. This *had* to be the poltergeist.

I stared at him. He stared back with bright, hard eyes. And I could suddenly feel how much he hated me. Wanted me gone.

I tore off the glasses and closed my eyes. My heart thudded in my chest. That feeling! How could anything hate me so much?

"Jill, what's wrong?" Freddy demanded. "What did you see?"

"The poltergeist," I croaked. "Over there, behind that box."

Freddy stared. "I don't see anything."

I peered into the gloom.

Neither did I! The poltergeist was gone!

Then I had a crazy idea. I handed Freddy the old-fashioned glasses. "Try these."

He slipped the glasses on. Meanwhile, I tried not to panic.

Freddy spoke softly. "I see it now! It's ugly, but it's small. Maybe we can catch it." He started toward the pile of boxes.

"Freddy, don't!" I shouted.

Too late. The trunk we had emptied earlier was already flying through the air! As I stared, it landed upside down with its lid open. Right on top of Freddy.

And then the trunk rolled over and scooped my little brother inside. *Slam!* The lid swung shut.

*"Freddy!"* I screamed. I sprang to the box and pulled frantically at the lid.

It wouldn't open!

I could hear my little brother thumping and yelling inside. "Freddy!" I called. "Push the lid! Push as hard as you can!"

Behind me came the whisper of things moving. I turned.

Oh, no!

The dressmaker's dummy had come back to life. And it wasn't alone. *All* of Uncle Solly's junk was on the move.

Books whipped down to whack my arms and legs. Scarves formed into bat shapes and hovered around my head. An army of plastic fingers scurried across the floor, stalking me.

"Leave me *alone!*" I yelled. I swiped at the books and bat things. They fluttered out of reach. Then I began to hit the trunk latch as hard as I could. I banged on it. I kicked it. I hammered it with my sneaker.

Finally it sprang open. I slammed up the lid, grabbed Freddy's hand, and pulled. "Come on. Run!"

We tore through the cloud of flying things. Plastic fingers crunched under our feet. Freddy yanked open the door while I whacked at a brown leather book that was dive-bombing me. We squeezed through the opening and pulled the door shut.

Then we dashed down the stairs, three at a time. We didn't stop until we got to my room and slammed the door behind us.

I threw myself on my bed, panting. "You saw the poltergeist," I said to Freddy.

Freddy nodded. "Yeah. With all that hair, and that weird pointy mouth, he looked like a cross between a monkey and a mosquito. A mean monkey," he added with a shiver.

He pulled the old-fashioned glasses out of his pocket and set them on my bed between us. We both stared at them for a second. How come we could see the poltergeist only when we were wearing them?

"You know they're magic glasses," Freddy said at last. It wasn't a question.

I nodded slowly. I had to admit it. Uncle Solly *did* have real magic!

"Now what?" Freddy asked.

I picked the glasses up and turned them over in my hands. "Well, with these at least we can *see* the poltergeist."

"Big deal. They didn't help us catch him," Freddy pointed out. "They didn't stop any bad stuff from happening."

I saw where he was heading. "We can't give up now!" I snapped at him. "There has to be a way to beat this thing."

Freddy shook his head. "We have to tell. Jill, the poltergeist is trying to get us. Aren't you even scared?"

I stared at him, shocked. "Are you kidding? Of course I'm scared. Who wouldn't be?"

"You don't act like it," Freddy told me. His round face was very serious. "You keep talking about how Mom loves this house, and we can't break her heart by telling her we have to move. But she loves us too. It would break her heart if something happened to *us*. And something almost happened just now. Up in the attic."

His words hit me hard. He was right. Maybe I should face facts. This thing was too powerful for me and Freddy to fight. We'd only lose.

I heard the front door open. Dad's cheery voice boomed through the house.

"Hi, all. The man is home!"

"You win," I said. "We'll tell them."

But could we make them believe us?

Or would they ground us for the next ten years?

"**P**oltergeists, huh? Sounds to me like somebody's got a case of Fear Street fever," Dad told us, grinning.

Freddy and I exchanged glances. Not a good start.

We were all gathered in the den. It was about nine-thirty that night. Freddy and I had decided to wait until after dinner to talk to Mom and Dad.

Dad started hunting around the couch. "Where's that remote control?" he asked. "I keep telling you kids to leave it on the coffee table."

"Dad," I pleaded. "Won't you listen?"

He raised his eyebrows. "Well, sure, pumpkin, I'll listen. Just as long as I don't have to believe." Even though Dad was born in Shadyside, his years in Texas left him with a drawl. He likes to pour it on even thicker than usual when he's joking with us.

He went back to hunting for the remote. "Ah, here it is, under the cushion. Of course, I know you kids didn't put it there. Probably that rascal poltergeist."

Mom sat in the chair next to the couch, looking annoyed. Neither of them believed a word we'd said.

"Why won't you believe us?" Freddy asked.

"Freddy, you forget, I was *there.*" Mom leaned forward, her eyes filled with concern. "I *heard* you wrestling before you broke the lamp. I saw the video of your uncle juggling those books, just the way you two did. And when I walked into that mess in the kitchen, all I saw were two kids whose horseplay had gotten out of hand."

"But the glasses—" I began.

"Ah, yes, the glasses," Dad said. "Let me see them."

I passed him the magic glasses. He slipped them on and peered around the room, searching. Suddenly his eyes widened. He gasped.

"Do you see it?" Freddy demanded.

"I do, I do," Dad cried. "By the fireplace. By golly, it's a snark! Right next to the frumious bander-snatch!"

"Dad!" I protested. He was treating the whole thing as a joke!

"And there's a rattlesnake, and the Cisco Kid," Dad went on. "And—why, I do believe that's a goblin! Eating a burrito."

Mom frowned. "There's no point in teasing them, John," she scolded.

"There's no point in them getting wrapped up in wild tales either," Dad replied. He slipped off the magic glasses and set them on the table.

"Look, kids," he went on in a more serious voice. "I remember what it was like when *I* was growing up in Shadyside. Kids at school told all kinds of stories about Fear Street. But in all my years here, I never met anyone this spooky stuff ever happened to first-hand. It was always 'a friend of a friend.' Which is usually a sure sign that a story isn't true."

"I can understand Freddy letting his imagination run away with him," Mom put in. "But you, Jill, are certainly old enough to know better."

I glanced over at Freddy. What were we going to do?

It wasn't fair. Parents never believe the really big stuff that happens to you. They always think you're exaggerating.

Oh, well. Maybe tomorrow we'd be able to think up a new plan. I sighed and got up to leave.

"Don't forget your glasses, Jill," Dad called after me. "What if you have a visitor?"

Silently, I walked back and picked up the specs. Freddy and I climbed the stairs as if we were marching to the hangman.

"I can't believe they just ignored us," Freddy complained. "I guess you were right, Jill. Sorry."

**60**

"Forget it," I advised. "No matter what Mom and Dad say, *we* know it's real. We just have to be on our guard from now on."

Using the glasses, Freddy and I did quick sweeps of both our bedrooms. Poltergeist free.

I went back to my room and put on my pajamas. Then I tottered down the hall to the bathroom to brush my teeth. I studied myself in the mirror as I gargled.

*Well, what now?* I asked myself.

I didn't have any good answers.

Back at my room, I hesitated at the door. Had I shut it? I didn't remember shutting it.

I turned the knob. The door swung wide.

I froze in horror.

In the doorway stood a huge yellow blob. It must have been seven feet tall. It *towered* over me. Its lumpy head had a wide, gaping black hole of a mouth.

A mouth that stretched even wider as the thing came after me!

# 12

I didn't even have time to scream. The monster's body wrapped around me. It was like being caught in a fishing net.

I struggled and beat at it. My heart raced. My stomach churned. I tried to call for help. But part of the yellow blob covered my mouth. It was tough to breathe, let alone yell.

The part around my legs suddenly tightened. I crashed to the floor. Help! I was being smothered!

I kicked, bit, and clawed. The thing was soft and yielding. Light filtered through its yellow sides. I felt as if I'd been swallowed by a tent.

Finally I clawed my way out. Free! Then I crawled away as fast as I could. The monster lay there, unmoving. Flat. Maybe I'd killed it!

Freddy dashed out of his room. "What was all that noise? And why is your bedspread lying out here in the hall?" he asked.

"Huh?" I stared at the yellow blob. Then, cautiously, I leaned over and prodded it.

Freddy was right. It was only my big yellow bedspread.

But a minute ago *it was coming after me!*

I grabbed the spread and climbed to my feet. "Follow me," I said.

While I told Freddy what had happened, I wadded the bedspread up and stuffed it into my closet. Then I realized I would spend the night waiting for it to come back *out* of the closet. So I tilted my dresser up and told Freddy to shove it under there.

"It'll get dirty," he objected.

"I hope it does," I retorted. "I hope it's afraid of the dark. I hope moths come and eat it in the middle of the night. Now shove it under there."

Freddy did as I asked. I lowered the dresser again. The bedspread fit nicely. Good thing it wasn't one of our thick winter comforters.

I was still shaking from my close call. *Three times in one day!* I thought. *How am I ever going to survive?*

"Freddy?" I said. "Can I sleep in your room tonight?"

Believe it or not, I had to talk him into it. Even though he has bunk beds! I guess it's because we had to wait so long to get our own rooms. But you'd think

**63**

he could have been a little more understanding. Especially after all we'd been through that day.

We stayed in our own rooms until Dad and Mom went to bed. No point trying to explain to *them*. Then I sneaked into Freddy's room.

He was sitting on the top bunk, his back against the wall. He clutched a baseball bat tightly in his hands. But he relaxed when I showed up.

"Do you want me to sleep on the bottom?" he asked.

"I don't care," I answered, yawning. "I'm so tired I could sleep standing up. It's been a long day."

"You ain't just a-woofin'," Freddy said.

I grinned to myself. That was one of Dad's expressions. It was kind of cute to hear it coming from the little Brainiac.

Time ticked along. But even though I felt wiped out, I couldn't fall asleep. Lying there in the dark, I heard every creak and groan in the old house. "Settling," Mom called it. But in the middle of the night, I wasn't so sure.

What was that creak? Was the poltergeist sneaking up on us now? If it could make dress dummies and bedspreads come to life, what else could it do? Could it take over our parents? Control them? Make them wander through the house like robots?

I shuddered and burrowed farther into the covers. Something hard poked my arm. I felt around and found the object. I peered at it in the dark.

The magic glasses!

But I'd left them in my room! I clearly remembered putting them down on my dresser. Right before I went to brush my teeth.

"Freddy?" I called softly.

No answer.

"Freddy, wake up." I reached up and gave him a shove.

"What?" He sat up, rubbing his eyes. "What is it? What?"

"The magic glasses," I said urgently. "Did you bring them in here from my room?"

Freddy leaned down from his bunk and grabbed his own glasses from the nightstand. "No."

"Well, why are they in my bunk, then?" I felt panic rising again, grabbing me by the throat.

*The glasses had moved on their own!*

"Maybe the poltergeist put them there," Freddy suggested.

Maybe. But why?

I slipped the glasses on and looked around the room. It was easy to see in the dark with them on. Another magic quality they had, I guess. No poltergeist in the room.

Then I heard another noise from downstairs. A new noise. The sound of something scraping, shuffling against the floor.

Something was down there. I was certain of it. Was it planning to get me and Freddy? Or Mom and Dad?

*Stay calm,* I told myself.

Yeah, right.

I pushed back the covers and climbed out of bed. "Get up," I ordered Freddy.

We couldn't just lie there in the dark, waiting for whatever it was to come get us. We had to *do* something.

Even if it meant risking our lives!

# 13

**W**e needed weapons. The best we could come up with was Freddy's baseball bat and my tennis racket. Oh, well, better than nothing. Holding them ready, we tiptoed down the hall.

I still had the magic glasses on. So I spotted him right away. The little hairy guy from the attic. Leaning calmly against the stair railing. He looked as if he was waiting for a bus.

I jumped forward and swatted at him.

He vanished! Just like that!

I spun around. "Where'd he go?" I asked softly.

*"Peeps,"* I heard in my ear.

"Ack!" I squawked. "Freddy! The poltergeist! He's on my shoulder!"

"Hold still!" Freddy ordered, and swung the bat.

I barely ducked in time to save my head. "Watch it, lamebrain!" I whispered furiously. "You almost decked me."

"I didn't mean to," he argued. "I can't see the stupid poltergeist, remember? I was just trying to help."

I reached up and felt my shoulder. Nothing there.

"Well, he's gone anyway," I said. "That's what matters. Now, for pete's sake, keep quiet. The last thing we need is for Mom and Dad to wake up and catch us out here. They'd ship us to the loony bin for sure."

We crept down the stairs. The poltergeist kept popping in and out of sight. Each time, I took a swing at him with my racket. And missed.

He was playing with us! The little creep!

When we reached the downstairs hall, the poltergeist stood on a chair. Waiting for us. His little black eyes glittered at me. I pounced and thwacked the racket on the seat of the chair.

Nothing.

"Did you get him?" Freddy asked.

"No," I growled. I flipped on a light.

"How come you keep missing?" Freddy wanted to know.

I gave him a look. "He keeps vanishing. How do you expect me to hit something that can just blink on and off like that? I think he pops from one place to another."

Then I heard *"Peeps"* again. And felt something land on my head. Oh, yuck!

**68**

I slowly raised my hands, trying to catch the little guy by surprise. All I caught was air.

Frustrated, I pulled off the glasses and handed them to Freddy. "Here, you try. Maybe you can do better. And use my racket instead of that bat. That way at least you won't kill *me* while you're trying to bean *him*."

Freddy leaned the bat against the wall and gave me his glasses to hold. Then he put on the magic glasses.

"There he goes!" he called immediately. He sped toward the den. I followed.

When I got there, I found Freddy standing still as a statue. The light was on—his hand was still on the switch. The tennis racket hung loose in his other hand.

All around us was that weird little sound: *"Peeps. Peeps. Peeeeeeps!"*

I felt cold. "What's going on?" I said. "Freddy, what's wrong?"

Silently, he handed me the glasses. I slipped them on.

And gasped.

*The room was filled with poltergeists!*

They sat on the bookshelves, and the television. They hung from the lamps, from the ceiling fan. They danced along the curtain rods. They bounced on the sofa cushions.

There were *dozens* of the little guys. Some were covered with brown hair. Some with black. Some with

**69**

red. Three or four were spotted, like Dalmatians. I even saw one with black-and-white zebra stripes. And all their tubelike mouths were working overtime. *"Peeps. Peeps. Peeeeps!"*

Then, all at once, every single one of them stopped *peepsing*. And turned to face us.

Slowly the little things made a circle, surrounding us. My knees shook so hard I thought I was going to fall over. I reached out and grabbed the back of a chair.

"Wh-why is it quiet all of a sudden?" Freddy stammered. Without the magic glasses, he was lost. "What's happening?"

"You don't want to know," I told him. "Just stick close to me."

The poltergeists' black eyes gleamed. The circle closed tighter. And they drew nearer.

Nearer.

This was the end! I shut my eyes. I didn't want to see.

Then a new sound broke the silence. A much uglier sound than the poltergeists' *peepsing*. It snarled and rumbled like nothing I'd ever heard.

My eyes flew open. I spun around, trying to see what it was.

Then I realized the sound came from outside the room.

But whatever made it was moving toward the den.

With a mad burst of *peepsing*, the poltergeists scattered. One leapt to an electric socket. I gasped as his body thinned, folded like paper, and squeezed through the tiny plug hole.

Others slipped like mist through cracks in the brick chimneypiece. One flattened itself and slid under the closet door. In a flash they were gone. We were alone.

The snarling noise grew louder. Clearly, whatever made that horrible sound had scared away all the poltergeists.

And if it could scare a poltergeist, what kind of horrible thing could *it* be?

Without realizing it, Freddy and I had backed up all the way to Mom's plate wall. Our backs were against it when a solid *thud* came from the other side. I could feel it all down my back.

Whatever was on the other side of that wall was powerful. And it was *coming after us!*

A horrible bubbling growl ripped the air.

"We've got to get out of here," I whispered.

Freddy didn't answer. He simply barreled out of the room.

"Wait for me!" I called, and tore out behind him.

We rushed up the stairs and into Freddy's room. I closed the door and turned the key in the lock.

"That should do it," I said. I moved into the room.

Freddy stared past me. "Look!" he whispered hoarsely. He pointed at the door.

I looked.

The doorknob was turning. All by itself.

# 14

We both stared at the turning doorknob. I felt helpless, like a bird facing a snake.

We were cornered. Was this the end? Were they coming for us?

I heard Freddy whimper behind me. He sounded really scared. Not that I could blame him. My heart thudded like crazy in my chest. I felt cold sweat trickle down my back.

And then the doorknob stopped moving.

My breathing stopped too, for a moment. I shoved the magic glasses up on my nose and stared at the crack under the door. Were poltergeists about to start popping through?

Or something *worse* than poltergeists?

But nothing happened. Nothing at all.

After about five minutes my muscles started to relax. Maybe we'd live until morning after all. Still, I didn't want to take too many chances. . . .

"I think we should keep watch," I told Freddy. "We'll take turns. I'll do the first watch. I'll wake you in an hour for the second. Deal?"

Freddy nodded gloomily. "Deal. But I'm too scared to fall asleep anyway."

"Try," I said, and patted him on the shoulder. Poor little Brainiac.

He climbed up to his bunk and lay down on top of the covers. I slid into the bottom bunk and leaned against the wall. I wore the magic glasses. I wanted to see them if they came.

The minutes slid by. I kept my eyes fixed on the door. My fingers clutched the baseball bat tightly. No way they were getting past me. No way. No way . . .

I woke up with a start at a peeping noise.

Hey! It was morning! Sun poured in the window. A robin perched on the sill, chirping. That must have been the sound that woke me.

I scrambled out of bed in a hurry. What if they'd come while I was sleeping? What if they'd done something horrible to Freddy?

But Freddy snored peacefully in his bunk. Whew! We'd survived the night.

I opened the door and peeped out. Everything seemed normal—at least in the upstairs hall.

Freddy made groggy waking noises. "What time is it? Is it my turn?" he murmured. Then he slid his glasses on. "Hey, it's morning! What happened?"

"I guess I fell asleep," I admitted. "Sorry. But we made it through the night anyhow."

Freddy blinked. "But what if they come back? What are we going to do?"

I bit my lip. "When we get home from school, let's try sticking close to Mom and Dad. Whatever they do, we do. If we're with them when the poltergeists come back, they'll *have* to believe us."

"What do we do when Mom and Dad go to bed?" Freddy asked.

"We'll wait until they're asleep and sneak in with them. We'll sleep on the floor if we have to."

Freddy swung his legs over the edge of the bunk and jumped to the floor. "I hope it works. I hope the poltergeists *do* try something in front of Mom and Dad. Because I get the feeling they aren't only trying to scare us."

I knew what Freddy meant. I could still see the poltergeists in my mind. Closing in on us. Their eyes gleaming. Their faces full of hate.

Freddy was right. They didn't just want to scare us.

They wanted to get rid of us!

# 15

At breakfast Mom cupped my chin in her hand and frowned. "Are you feeling all right?" she asked. "You're a bit pale."

I stared at my plate. "I didn't sleep too well."

Mom clucked her tongue. "Did you stay up late reading those scary books again? I've warned you about that, Jill. No wonder you're imagining poltergeists."

I didn't say anything. What good would it do?

I stumbled through school that day in a daze. Who knows what kind of dumb things I said in class. I couldn't concentrate. I didn't even notice if anyone made fun of me.

I couldn't stop thinking about tonight. I had a

feeling tonight would be the end of it. One way or another.

Finally the school day was over. Freddy and I walked home together.

When we reached our house, we stood on the lawn for a minute. Staring at it.

"It looked so cool when we got here," Freddy said sadly.

I nodded. It had seemed like such a great place to live.

But not anymore. Now it looked dark, mean. The windows glared down at us in the afternoon sun. The door stood waiting. Ready to open and swallow us whole.

I hitched my backpack up and stepped forward. "Remember our plan," I warned Freddy. "Whatever Mom does, we stick with her. If she's cooking, we help her cook. If she's reading, we get a book and join her. We don't let her out of our sight."

"I know," Freddy answered. "She won't get away from *me.*"

As soon as we walked through the front door I put the magic glasses on. No poltergeists in the hall.

"Mom?" I called. "We're home."

Silence answered me.

Freddy slid off his backpack and let it drop by the hall table. "Isn't she here?" he asked nervously.

"Maybe she's upstairs, or in the basement." I tried to sound reassuring. "Mom!" I called again, louder.

**76**

Still no answer.

"She probably ran to the store or something," Freddy suggested. His voice shook a little.

We found her note in the kitchen, beside a vase of flowers.

*Jill and Freddy,*

*Dad surprised me with flowers this afternoon. It's the anniversary of the day we met. Isn't he sweet! We're off to dinner and a movie. Back by eleven. There's a lasagna in the oven. Don't get into mischief.*

*Love, Mom*

"So much for the great plan," Freddy groaned. "Now what are we going to do? We're all alone!"

He looked as if he was about to cry. I licked my lips, trying to think of something to cheer him up. And to cheer *me* up, if you want the truth. We had a long, scary evening to get through! Somehow, we had to pass the time. And then I got an idea.

I started rummaging through the cupboards. "We'll have our own party!" I exclaimed. I threw a bag of popcorn in the microwave. I got a tray out and piled it with cookies and M&Ms. When the microwave dinged, I poured the hot popcorn into a big bowl. I put it in the center of the tray.

"Ta-da!" I sang, plopping the tray in front of

Freddy. "I declare today official Pig-Out Day! Grab some sodas and let's take this stuff to the den."

Freddy's eyes lit up at the sight of all that junk food. Mom wouldn't like it, but I didn't care. This was an emergency.

In the den I set the tray on the coffee table.

"What are we going to do?" Freddy asked.

"Let's watch that video of Uncle Solly again," I told him. "Remember how much fun it was?"

Freddy took the tape from the closet and we slipped it into the VCR. We plopped onto the couch to watch.

I'd forgotten I was still wearing the magic glasses. But the moment Uncle Solly started doing his tricks, I remembered. Boy, did I remember!

My mouth fell open in shock. I slipped the glasses on and off again. Could I really be seeing what I was seeing?

"What's the matter with you?" Freddy asked, staring at me.

"Th-the video," I stuttered. "It's different!"

With the glasses on, everything had changed. All around Uncle Solly, perched on his table and his shoulders and at the end of his magic wand, were—

Poltergeists!

# 16

The hairy little creatures jumped and capered across the TV screen. And their faces! They looked so different from my memories of last night. They were cheerful. Even cute!

I handed the glasses to Freddy. His eyes grew round as he watched. He grabbed my arm.

"That's it! Don't you see?" he practically yelled. "That's how come Uncle Solly's magic looked so real. Because it *was* real! It's poltergeist magic!"

I gasped.

If Freddy was right, the poltergeists weren't haunting Uncle Solly. Not at all.

*They were helping him!*

I took the glasses back and stared at the screen.

It was true! Everywhere a fishbowl or a box hung in

the air, there was a poltergeist underneath it, pointing at it.

The poltergeists were helping Uncle Solly do his act!

" 'Take care of the little people,' " I murmured.

"Huh?" Freddy asked.

"What Uncle Solly used to say. 'Take care of the little people and you're set for life.' He was trying to tell us, Freddy," I said slowly. "The poltergeists— they must be the little people he meant. Uncle Solly knew we'd move to this house someday when he was gone."

"You mean he wanted us to make *friends* with the poltergeists?" Freddy demanded.

I nodded. My mind was working on overdrive.

Maybe we'd been wrong about this whole thing from the beginning. Maybe the hairy little men weren't poltergeists at all! After all, a poltergeist is a kind of ghost, right? These creatures didn't seem like ghosts to me. Magic, yes. Spirits—no. These little guys were very much alive.

This changed everything. If we were right about who the little people were—and if we could make friends with them—we wouldn't have to be afraid. Mom could keep her house. We could all stay here together!

Then I noticed a long, thin stream of mist. It leaked upward from the tiny crack between two floorboards.

The stream wavered, swelled. Then it formed into the shape of a little man!

One by one, they appeared around us. One slipped like slime from a wall plug. It slopped out in a pool on the floor. The head and then the shoulders and finally the rest of the creature emerged from the pool. This one had red hair with black speckles.

Another shot like a laser beam from the light switch. It bounced around the room. Then it stopped suddenly. A fresh, whole creature balanced on the edge of our popcorn bowl. Its gaze was glued to the television screen.

"Freddy," I whispered. "They're here."

Soon there were dozens of them in the room. They perched on lamps and chairs and tables, all watching the videotape with sad expressions on their tiny faces.

Freddy and I took turns watching them through the glasses. They paid no attention to us at all.

Then they started making those noises again. *Peeps, peeps, peeeeps.* This time though, they sounded different to us.

"I—I think they're crying," Freddy whispered.

"Me too," I agreed. "They must miss Uncle Solly."

"Maybe they don't understand why he's gone," Freddy said.

"Maybe." That gave me an idea. "And maybe that's why they've been so mean to us! They think we're intruders."

How could we make friends with them?

Then I got another idea.

"Freddy," I whispered. "Go get your magic stuff. Put on your cape and your top hat. Then bring your tricks back down here."

"Why?" Freddy asked. Then his eyes lit up. "Oh, I get it."

He slipped quietly out of the room. I heard him running up the stairs to his room. The creatures were so wrapped up in Uncle Solly's video, they didn't even seem to notice.

I was alone. Surrounded by little people. The hair rose all over my arms and legs. "Hurry, Freddy," I whispered through clenched teeth.

Nervously I grabbed an Oreo off the tray. I wasn't even hungry. It was more like I wanted something to do.

I heard a curious *peeps* in my ear.

My gaze slid to the side. I caught my breath. There was a tiny man on my shoulder! It was the zebra-striped one I'd noticed earlier.

He stared curiously at my cookie. He didn't seem threatening. I held the cookie up for him to inspect.

The creature blinked rapidly. Then he poked his tubelike mouth into the cookie and began slurping the filling out of the center.

He didn't stop until all the creamy filling was gone. Then he sat back and starting *peepsing* happily. His

**82**

little eyes gleamed. But for some reason they didn't scare me anymore.

My heart beat fast. We *could* make friends with them!

Freddy stepped into the den, decked out in his magician's outfit. His top hat sat at a tilt on his head.

"Should I start now?" he asked.

"No, let the video finish," I decided. "They might get mad if we turn it off."

Freddy sat back down and watched. When the tape reached the part with the puppet in the box, the little people began *peepsing* like crazy and pointing to the screen. I could have sworn I saw fear on their little faces. What could that mean?

The video finally ended. The creatures began jabbering again. I poked Freddy.

"Now," I said.

Freddy swallowed hard. He stood in front of the TV and announced in a shaky voice, "Ladies and gentlemen, the great Frederico!"

He bowed and waved his wand.

The little people stopped *peepsing* and watched him with bright, curious eyes.

"See?" Freddy said. "Nothing in my hands. And nothing up my sleeve." He wiped his hands together, made a fist of one, then produced a handkerchief from his fist.

But Freddy was nervous. He fumbled it. The

plastic thumb he'd hidden the silk in fell from his hand and bounced on the floor.

A loud chorus of *peepsing* followed that. The little guys rolled around, holding their bellies and chirping.

"What are they doing?" Freddy asked.

I grinned. "I think they're laughing at you."

Freddy blushed and pulled out a deck of cards. He made a fan with the cards. But once again he fumbled it. The entire deck spilled to the floor!

Freddy looked miserable. He was proud of his act. But he was just too nervous to get it right.

The little people didn't seem to mind though. They thought he was a riot!

Then one of them jumped and landed on Freddy's shoulder.

"Freddy," I said quietly, "one of them is sitting on you. Wave your hand at the cards on the floor and see what happens."

Freddy held out a shaking hand, passed it above the cards, and said, "Abracadabra!"

The creature flicked his fingers. The cards shot up from the floor and smacked Freddy square in the nose.

"Ow!" He rubbed his nose, glaring at me.

Uh-oh! "Don't get mad," I warned him. "Laugh like it's a great joke."

"Ha-ha," Freddy said halfheartedly.

"Louder!" I insisted. "Make it sound like you mean it."

To help him out, I laughed too. At first it was hard. But then the whole situation struck us just right. Suddenly, we were laughing for real.

The little guys *peepsed* happily. More of them jumped on Freddy. The cards began to dance around him in the air. He waved his hands. The cards followed his movements!

"Wow!" he declared. I clapped my hands.

The creatures helped Freddy with trick after trick. In no time, they lost all their shyness. They swung from our fingers. They danced up and down our arms.

This is great! I thought. Our troubles are over. We'll never have to be scared again!

Boy, was I wrong.

In the middle of Freddy's act, a shuddering howl ripped through the air. My breath caught in my throat. Fear turned my backbone to a blade of ice.

*What was that?*

The little people froze in their tracks. We all stared in terror at the open den door.

From the hallway something tumbled into the room.

Something blue.

It was no bigger than a basketball. It stood on crooked hind legs. Its long arms were covered with matted blue fur.

The thing raised its hairy arms and shrieked. Claws glinted in the light. Red eyes smoldered from the matted hair of its face. Slime dripped from its long, greenish fangs. The slime smoked and hissed where it hit the floor.

I gasped. I'd seen this nightmare before. Only a few minutes ago, as a matter of fact.

It was the evil-looking puppet from the box.

But it was no puppet.

It was alive!

# 17

**"T**he puppet. It's real!" Freddy shrieked.

Apparently, he didn't need magic glasses to see the thing. At the sound of his voice, the monster scuttled toward Freddy. It moved like a monkey, flinging its arms. Then it reared up and swiped at my little brother.

"Aaagh!" Freddy yelled, and jumped away.

Little people were leaping everywhere in total panic. One of them rode Freddy's shoulder, holding on for grim life.

Where had the evil thing come from? A picture suddenly flashed through my mind. Of the box clattering on the attic floor. And the sound of air—or *something*—whooshing out.

I grabbed the nearest thing I could find and threw it. It was an Oreo. The monster snatched it out of the air and gulped it down.

A moment later its face twisted into an even uglier expression. It started heaving. Then it threw up the cookie and a pool of purple gunk all over the floor.

"Oh, gross me out!" I groaned.

The monster snarled at me. Its mouth gaped, a hideous hole at least half the size of its head.

"Hey! Where did it go?" Freddy shouted.

"Can't you see it? It's there, to your left," I called, pointing.

"No." He looked panicky. "I can't see it. It must be able to make itself disappear!"

"I can still see it with these glasses," I said grimly.

I glanced around for something I could use as a weapon. There was nothing.

Suddenly the monster lunged toward Freddy.

"Freddy!" I yelled. Without thinking, I leapt and tackled the creature. My leg twisted under me as I landed. I winced at the sudden stab of pain.

The thing was much smaller than me, but heavy. Its fur felt greasy and coarse. And the smell! Like garbage on a hot day. I rolled with it, then threw it as hard as I could at the wall.

The monster hit the wall with a heavy thud. It slid to the floor. And lay there. Still.

I got up, wiping my hands on my jeans. But the

greasy feeling wouldn't go away. *Or* the smell. I was afraid I was going to be sick.

I took a step. Pain shot through the leg I'd twisted. Oh, no! This was horrible. How could I get away?

"Freddy, I'm hurt," I gasped.

He dashed to my side. "Can you run?" he asked.

I gritted my teeth. "I'll try."

Freddy slipped his arm under mine to help take the weight off my leg. We staggered to the door. Little people bounced off the walls around us. I wondered why they didn't simply vanish. They seemed crazy with fear.

"RRRRROWWWRRR!"

My stomach lurched. I glanced over my shoulder.

The monster had come out of its daze. It crept after us. Its eyes glowed at me with a sick hunger.

I was prey—and the prey was lame. It was only a matter of time.

"Hurry, Freddy," I moaned. "He's following us."

"I'm trying," my brother grunted.

We dragged ourselves into the hall. My injured leg banged against the hall table. I couldn't help jerking. It hurt so much!

"Whoa!" Freddy yelled. He lost his balance. The two of us toppled to the floor.

"Oh," I groaned. Aching and trembling, I pushed myself up. I couldn't see the monster. Frantic, I swept the hallway with the magic glasses.

There! There it was! Sneaking up behind the table. Less than a yard away!

I felt helpless. A look of glee crossed the monster's face.

Before it could move another step, a playing card whacked it in the face.

It growled and backed up. Another struck it, and another.

Freddy! He was whizzing his deck of cards at the monster. They flew out of his hands at dizzying speed.

"Go, Brainiac!" I cheered.

"I'm judging where it is by the stink!" he yelled to me. "And you laughed at me when I showed you that book on using cards as weapons."

"I'll never laugh again!" I promised.

But then a look of horror crossed his face. He searched frantically in his pockets.

Oh, no!

Freddy had run out of cards!

The monster crept forward again. Snarling. Drooling.

The tiny guy on Freddy's shoulder *peepsed* like crazy. Then I noticed that all the other little people had come out of hiding. They danced around the monster. They snapped their tiny fingers in front of its hideous nose.

All at once I realized what they were doing. They were trying to distract the monster.

That's why they hadn't just vanished.

They were trying to save us!

The monster went mad with rage! It swatted in every direction at the dancing little people.

"Let's get out of here, Freddy," I whispered. "While the little guys distract him."

Freddy helped me to my feet again. "Where to?"

"The kitchen." I knew we could find something to fight the monster in there. Knives, pots and pans, the sprayer from the sink. In the kitchen we might have a chance.

We were at the kitchen door, when we heard a *peepsing* scream behind us. I spun around.

The monster had caught one of the little people! My zebra-striped friend! It clutched the tiny man in its taloned paw and grinned wickedly at me.

"What's happening? What?" wailed Freddy.

"You don't want to know," I whispered. Now I *really* felt sick.

Without taking its eyes from mine, the monster tossed the little man into its mouth.

And swallowed him.

Whole.

# 18

**"N**o!" I screamed.

Too late. The little man was gone.

Freddy and I pushed through the kitchen door. I collapsed onto a chair. I tried to ignore the sounds of the monster snarling and swiping at the little people in the hall.

"Oh, Freddy," I moaned. "How could we have been so wrong about the little people? That poor guy gave his life to save us."

Freddy's face was the color of milk. "What are we going to do, Jill?" he whispered.

I clutched my head in my hands. Think, Jill!

Uncle Solly had been able to control the monster somehow. But we weren't Uncle Solly. He'd been a trained magician. We were just a couple of kids.

We'd have to fight it the old-fashioned way.

"A knife," I told Freddy. "Find me Mom's biggest knife. And bring me the big skillet from the cabinet by the window."

Freddy dashed around the kitchen, finding the things I'd asked for. The knife he brought me was huge—maybe ten inches long. And the skillet was so heavy, I couldn't hold it for too long.

I lined my weapons up on the table in front of me.

"What are you going to do?" Freddy asked.

I grabbed his arm. "I want you to run. Now, while the little people are still keeping that thing busy. Flag down a police car. Or find a neighbor. Or *anyone*. Just get help."

Freddy's mouth set in a stubborn line. "What about you? I'm not leaving you here."

"You have to," I insisted. "I can't run. But I'll be okay. I can see the thing with the glasses, remember? And we know it can be hurt." I laid a hand on the frying pan. "If it comes near me, I'll wallop it into next week. Don't worry. I'll be fine."

I hoped I looked more confident than I felt. I wasn't at all sure I could hold out against the monster. Especially when I couldn't even walk!

But even if I didn't make it, maybe Freddy could.

He shook his head. "I won't do it. You need me."

"Hey! Just who's the older sister here anyway?" I demanded. I made my voice gruff so he couldn't hear

**93**

the way it shook. "You have to do it. Promise me." I shook him hard. *"Promise me!"*

Slowly, he nodded. He wiped a pudgy hand across his face.

"Maybe the monster won't even come in here," he said. "Maybe it's full."

I listened. The monster had gone quiet.

Somehow, that was worse than the snarling. What had it done to the little people? Eaten them all?

We sat tense. Every so often, shuffling sounds drifted in from the other room. Like talons scraping on the floor.

"What's it doing?" Freddy whispered.

"Who knows? It's smart," I pointed out. "It's probably planning some kind of strategy. Here, help me move this chair away from the table."

We got me positioned with a straight shot at the door. I wanted to be the first thing it saw when it came through. If I could just get close enough to grab it . . .

Then I could make sure Freddy had the time to get away.

The seconds ticked by in silence.

Suddenly I heard a frantic clatter of talons on wood.

An instant later a ball of greasy blue fur shot through the door.

The monster! It tore straight at me.

I snatched the knife off the table. "Run, Freddy!" I shouted.

The creature hit me full in the chest. I fell backward, chair and all, to the floor.

Freddy streaked out of the kitchen.

The monster clawed at my arms and head. I swiped at it with the knife. Snarling, it walloped my hand.

"Ow!" I howled with pain. The knife flew out of my grasp and clattered across the floor.

What now? I was so scared, I didn't even think. I just hauled off and punched the monster in its furry blue stomach.

It gagged. And the little zebra-striped man came popping out of its mouth!

The poor little guy was covered in slime. You could barely make out his stripes. But he was alive and well! He fled across the floor.

"Go on, little guy!" I yelled.

I punched the monster again.

"GNNNNNARRR!" it howled. Clawed fingers snatched for my eyes. I pulled back.

But not fast enough. The monster's claws ripped the glasses right off my face.

In despair I watched them fly across the room. They hit the wall. And shattered into a zillion pieces.

"No!" I shouted. "No! No!"

Without the glasses I couldn't see the monster. It could be anywhere. Sneaking up behind me.

I was finished!

# 19

Without the glasses I was blind! Where was the monster?

I could hear its claws on the kitchen tile. Closer. Closer. It seemed to be taking its time. Making me sweat.

Frantic, I scooted over to the kitchen counter. I grabbed one of the cabinet door pulls and tried to haul myself up.

I felt a *whoosh. Eau de garbage* filled my nostrils. The monster must have leapt past me to the counter-top.

Something sticky and repulsive swept over my cheek. The thing was licking me! I screeched with terror and leapt nearly all the way across the room. Bad leg and all!

I huddled against the far wall, frantically rubbing at the gunk the monster's slimy tongue had left on my face. I gagged at the feel of it. Cold and slimy. And it *really* reeked.

I heard the monster skittering across the countertop. A drawer opened. And a shish-kebab skewer rose into the air.

It hovered for a minute, then arrowed through the air. Straight at me! I yelled and shut my eyes.

*Thoink!*

Was I a shish kebab? I didn't feel any pain. Cautiously, I opened my eyes and looked to the right, where the sound had come from.

The skewer had pinned my shirtsleeve to the wall.

I yanked my shirt free. The monster is playing with me, I thought. It's enjoying itself. Like a cat playing with a mouse. Only I'm the mouse!

I climbed painfully to my feet. Where was the vicious thing? I couldn't hear its clattering claws anymore.

I eyed the doorway. Maybe I could get away! I lunged for it.

Invisible claws raked across my ankle. I stumbled and cracked my chin on the tile floor. Tears of pain rose in my eyes.

Invisible hands grabbed my ankles and dragged me, screaming, back to the sink. The monster was so strong!

And then I heard it smack its lips.

I scrambled to my feet. Greasy, ropy arms wrapped around my knees, trying to drag me down. I scanned the counter desperately. There must be something I could use as a weapon.

My gaze fell on the flour canister. A picture flashed through my mind. Tiny tracks in the powder on my dresser.

I had an idea.

It could work only if Mom had refilled the flour canister since the pie-making disaster. Please, please, I begged silently. I grabbed the canister and ripped the lid off.

I practically sobbed with relief when I saw the fluffy white powder inside.

Then I dumped the whole canister right on the monster as it squeezed my knees.

Direct hit! Flour burst around the thing. I could see it again! The flour clung to its greasy fur. It looked like a deranged pom-pom. With fangs. And claws.

The monster coughed and wiped at its eyes. I grabbed Mom's marble rolling pin from the counter. With all my strength I whacked the monster.

I was so frantic that my aim wasn't perfect. The blow landed on the thing's shoulder instead of its head. But it let go of my legs with a howl.

I kicked it away from me. Ow! I'd used my bad leg by accident. Pain seared through my knee.

The creature lay in the middle of the floor, stunned.

I limped forward to finish it off. I raised the roller high.

But I didn't have the strength to hit the monster again. My muscles gave way. I dropped the rolling pin and crumpled to the floor.

The monster groaned. Stirred.

I stared at it. Helpless. I couldn't get away. I couldn't move. My strength was gone.

Pinpricks of red light shone through the matted fur of the monster's face. Eyes. They glinted evilly at me.

The monster was waking up!

# 20

The monster climbed to its feet and shook itself. Clouds of flour burst from it. But I could still see it just fine.

It wasn't a pretty sight.

The monster quivered with rage.

And then it started to change!

Its face grew leaner and sharper. Its eyes bulged. Sharp thorns burst from its hairy arms. It made a fist. When it opened its hand again, the claws were longer, sharper than before.

"Oh, no," I whispered. It was really over now. I was a goner for sure.

I closed my eyes, waiting for the end.

Then I heard a burst of noise. *"Peeps! Peeps! PEEEEPS!"*

The little people! The monster hadn't scarfed them all down. And they were back!

I opened my eyes again. Something was hovering in the air near my head. A wooden box.

The puppet box! The little people must have brought it from the attic!

The monster spotted the box too. The sight seemed to put it in an even worse mood than before. It roared and bounded toward me.

Then a voice from the kitchen doorway made it stop in mid-bound.

"Hey, monster!"

Freddy! I couldn't believe it. My little brother stood in the doorway. He was wearing his Dallas Cowboys football helmet and pads. He held his baseball bat ready to swing.

He looked completely ridiculous. And I was never so glad to see him in my life!

The monster screeched with rage and leapt at Freddy.

"Batter up!" Freddy yelled. He swung the wooden bat.

*Crrrrrrck!* The bat whacked the monster square in the chest.

Wood splintered. And the bat snapped in half!

Oh, no!

The monster tumbled backward, end over end. Toward me.

**101**

I snatched up the marble rolling pin from the floor. This time I didn't plan to miss.

*Wham!* I brought the rolling pin down on the thing's head with everything I had.

The monster grunted and fell. Out cold.

*"Peeps!"* the little people sang. The puppet box fell to the floor beside me.

I scooped up the greasy, stinking, floury monster, shoved it inside, and slammed the lid.

Then I collapsed on the floor.

Freddy rushed over to me. "Are you all right?" he cried. "I thought that thing was going to kill you!"

"I'm fine," I wheezed. "Thanks to the little people—and you!" Then I frowned. "Hey, I thought I told you to run."

He grinned. He looked goofy with the helmet on. "Would the Dallas Cowboys run?"

I laughed. My Brainiac brother. He was all right!

A tinkling sound filled the air. Freddy and I turned.

Thousands of tiny bits from the broken glasses rose into the air. The wire frames floated beside them. Then, in a flash of light, the pieces all fused together.

The glasses were whole again.

They floated across the room to me. I put them on.

The little people were grouped around us, beaming. I waggled my fingers at them. "Hi, guys. And thanks a million!"

The striped one jumped into my lap. *"Peeps!"* he trilled.

"Well, I guess that's—" I started to say.

A noise from the box interrupted me.

The monster was beating against the lid!

The box banged and jumped on the floor. The broken clasp shook. Wiggled.

The monster was trying to break out!

# 21

![decorative flourish]

**"O**h, no, you don't!" I yelled.

I scrambled up and threw myself on the box. I could feel the monster pounding against the lid. *Whack! Whack!*

"Quick!" I told Freddy. "Find some wire or something to hold the latch closed."

"Right!" Freddy said. "Just don't let it out."

"Well, duh!" I snapped. "Will you please hurry?"

Freddy ran out. I clutched the box grimly.

*Whack! Whack! Whack!* Each time the monster hit the lid, the whole box jumped off the floor. But I was ready for it. I sat on that box and rode it like a rodeo queen. No way was that furry freak going to get past *me*. I wasn't about to go through that nightmare again!

At last Freddy ran back in. He waved a padlock at me. "I got it out of Dad's tool kit," he panted.

He slipped the lock through the latch and clicked it shut.

Silence. Immediately the monster stopped struggling.

Together we sat on the floor, our backs to the cabinets. We were totally beat.

"We did it, Jill!" Freddy crowed.

I glanced at my little brother. His eyes shone with excitement. I was happy too. But mostly I was exhausted.

And there was one more thing I needed to do.

I pointed at the padlocked box. "Do you feel comfortable with that?" I asked Freddy.

He made a face. "Not really."

I got to my feet and limped into the garage. I fetched the hammer and some finishing nails from Dad's tool kit. Then I nailed the box lid shut. Just in case.

We carried the box back up to the attic and shoved it behind the biggest pile of trunks. We didn't want Mom or Dad finding it and opening it!

"That should do it," I said.

"Maybe so. But if we spot any new buildings going up around here, let's dump the box into the wet concrete," Freddy answered. He wasn't smiling.

We went back downstairs. Dozens of little people

flitted after us, *peepsing* like crazy. Apparently they approved of us.

I thought of something. "Maybe that's how Uncle Solly made friends with them in the first place," I suggested. "Maybe this monster is their enemy. But he captured it. Just like we did."

In the kitchen I gazed at the mess on the floor. Flour lay everywhere. The shish-kebab skewer had left a hole in the wall. Chairs were knocked over.

And the den! What kind of mess would we find in there? I thought of the pool of monster puke. Oh, gross! I was going to have to clean *that* up?

Little people *peepsed* away on the kitchen table. I frowned thoughtfully, then held out my hand. A creature stepped onto my palm—the brown one we saw in the attic. I put him on my shoulder.

"What do you say, little guy?" I asked him. "Can you help us with this mess?"

*"Peeps!"*

I pointed to the flour, then to the canister.

*"Peeps! Peeps!"*

The little man waved his hands. Flour rose in a white tornado. Flecks of dust and dirt and monster filth spun away and formed a second, dirty twister.

The flour spun itself back into the canister. The filth spun straight into the garbage.

I picked up the canister and sniffed the flour. Fresh and perfect!

"Excellent!" I exclaimed.

After that the other little people got into the act. The knife returned to its drawer. So did the skewer. The skillet sailed back into the cabinet. And the holes in the wall filled themselves in before our eyes! Grains of plaster dust leapt up from the floor and into the dents. It was like watching a videotape on rewind.

We wandered through the house. Everywhere we passed, the little people did their thing. And everything they touched was left cleaner and brighter than before.

In no time the whole house was spotless. Freddy and I stood in the den. We stared at each other in delight.

"You guys are the greatest," I told the creatures. "You know, you could make a lot of money as a cleaning service!"

Just then the front door opened. Mom and Dad walked in.

"I hope they haven't been up to any more roughhousing," Mom was saying. "And all that nonsense about poltergeists! I'm a little worried about them, frankly."

"I don't think it's that serious," Dad replied.

We met them at the door to the den. Mom gazed around in wonder.

"Well, I'll be. You cleaned up." She ran her finger across some shelves. "Boy, did you clean up! This is more like it." Then she narrowed her eyes at us. "Did Dad put you up to this?"

I laughed. "No! We just thought—you know. Special day and all."

Mom still looked suspicious. "Well, I hope you at least had a little fun. What else did you do?"

"Watched a video," I told her.

She sighed. "TV. I wish you kids would find something active to do. What about school sports? Otherwise you're going to be a couple of couch potatoes."

That was too much for Freddy. *"Active?"* he sputtered. "You want to hear about active?"

I kicked the back of his leg. He stopped.

"We'll try," I said to Mom.

Her face broke into a smile. She pulled Freddy and me to her and hugged us. "I know you will. And I know we're all going to be very happy," she said. "Don't you just love this house?"

Freddy and I exchanged glances.

"Yeah," I said. "I think we do."

Freddy and I said our good nights and headed up to bed. As soon as we were out of the room, I slipped the magic glasses on. A tiny hairy man bowed politely to us from the banister.

"One good thing about this house," I said. "From now on, chores are going to be a snap!"

# 22

The next morning I waved to Freddy as he walked off to his own school. Two little people sat happily on his shoulders. The kids in his class were going to get a pretty special magic show, I guessed. Bullies might get a surprise as well.

I had just met up with Breanna outside the middle school when someone tapped my shoulder. I turned. Breanna's brother, Bobby, stood behind me.

He grinned at me. "What's happening, Tex?"

"Hi, Bobby," I said cautiously. I still wasn't sure how to take him.

Bobby turned to his sister. "Did you ask her yet?"

"I haven't had a chance," Breanna protested. "You ask."

Bobby turned back to me. "Will you come to our party?" he asked.

I felt my cheeks turning pink. "You're having a party?"

"Next Friday," Breanna confirmed.

"And I'm invited?" I blurted out.

"Well, of course you are!" Breanna answered, laughing. "All our friends are invited."

*Friends,* she said.

I beamed. "I'd love to come," I told them both.


Later that day I took my seat in science class. Mrs. McCord wrote busily at the blackboard.

I slipped on my special glasses and pointed to her. The little zebra-striped man on my shoulder nodded and jumped away.

The chalk broke in Mrs. McCord's hand. She picked up another stick.

It broke too. Then another. And another.

Finally, Mrs. McCord gave up. "I don't understand it," she murmured, looking puzzled. "Whoever heard of rotten chalk?"

I slipped the glasses back in my knapsack and stood up. "Let me help you, Mrs. McCord," I called.

Mrs. McCord peered over her glasses at me. "I beg your pardon?"

I went to the chalkboard and grabbed a piece of chalk. "What do you want me to write?" I asked.

"Thanks for offering, Jill, but the chalk is no good," Mrs. McCord said, smiling.

I shrugged. "It feels fine to me." I grabbed her notes and started writing away. I could feel everyone staring at me.

After a moment of trouble-free writing, the teacher said, "Let me see that chalk."

I handed her the stick I'd been using. She stared at it suspiciously. Then she started to write.

The chalk broke.

She started again.

The chalk broke again.

"Try another piece," I suggested. I picked one up from the tray under the blackboard. I wrote my name in big, loopy letters. "See? Piece of cake." I smiled.

Mrs. McCord snatched the chalk from me. It broke as soon as it touched the board.

People started giggling.

I grabbed another and showed that it, too, was fine.

Mrs. McCord tried it. It broke.

By now kids were rolling in the aisles. Mrs. McCord's face was red. "Now, why can't I—" she began.

Then she broke off and narrowed her eyes at me.

I turned to the class and hooked my mouth with my finger. "Caught you like a fish!" I said.

The class howled.

At first I was afraid Mrs. McCord wasn't going to

be a good sport. But finally she burst out laughing. "Nice one, Jill. How on earth did you do it?" she asked me.

I just grinned and shrugged.

On my way back to my desk I pointed at Bobby. "You're next," I told him.

Bobby groaned and slumped lower in his seat.

At my left ear I heard a tiny voice: *"Peeps?"*

"Soon, little friend," I whispered. "Very, very soon."

I turned to Bobby and smiled my biggest, fakest smile. He was about to be very impressed with the tricks I had up my sleeve.

Or—to be precise—sitting on my shoulder!

Are you ready for another walk
down Fear Street?
Turn the page for a terrifying
sneak preview.

R.L.STINE'S

GHOSTS OF FEAR STREET® #18

CAMP FEAR GHOULS

Coming mid-February 1997

I stood a few yards to the side of the cemetery gate. One rickety old house stood directly in front of me. It had lots of carved wooden decorations around the porch. From the walkway I could see the huge spider-webs that hung off them.

The front steps were splintered and sagging. The screen on the front door hung open on one twisted hinge. The weeds sprouting from the lawn were nearly as tall as me.

I read the address out loud: "Three three three."

I thought the Camp Fear Girls' invitation said 333. But that couldn't be right.

I thought we would be meeting at the house of one of the members. But no one could possibly live here. This place was a wreck!

I dug into the pocket of my jacket and pulled out my invitation. Even in the dim light, it was easy to read the big bold numbers. *333.*

Yes. This was definitely the right address.

"Weird," I murmured, making my way up the broken steps.

*Creak!*

A board bent under my foot. It began to splinter and crack. I jumped forward.

*CRRRACK!* The board snapped in half.

Whoa! This is dangerous, I realized. My foot could have gone right through!

I stepped carefully over to a nearby window and peered inside. I couldn't see anything. The glass was caked with dust and cobwebs, inside and out.

Then I moved to the door. I knocked gently.

*Tap. Tap. Tap.*

Strange laughter floated from inside the old house. It sounded warped. Slowed down. Like a tape recorder with its batteries running low.

I shivered. Who—or what—could laugh like that?

I froze, listening. I couldn't hear anyone coming to the door.

I took a shaky breath. I slowly reached out and rapped on the door again. This time harder.

*Ha ha ha ha ha.*

I shuddered. That creepy laughter again! And still no one came to the door.

Something was wrong here. Very wrong.

I *had* to be at the wrong place.

"I'm out of here," I declared loudly. "Who needs the Camp—"

My words died in my throat. An icy cold hand gripped my shoulder!

I spun around. And saw Amy!

"You scared me!" I gasped.

"That was the idea," Amy told me, wiggling her eyebrows.

She was dressed in a dark blue pleated skirt and white blouse, with a red bandanna around her neck. A matching red sash with several rows of badges sewn to it hung across her chest.

"Why are you standing out here?" Amy asked. "Wouldn't they let you in?"

I shook my head. "I wasn't sure I was at the right place. I could hear people laughing inside, but nobody answered when I knocked."

Amy slapped her forehead with the palm of her hand. "Oh, that's right—you don't know the secret knock."

She crossed to the door and tapped three times, slowly. Then two times fast, and then three more times slowly.

The front door creaked open.

"See?" Amy shrugged. "Nothing to it."

I followed Amy through the darkened entry. I turned to see who had opened the door.

There was no one there! Did the door open all by itself?

No. That was dumb. The door had probably been unlatched all this time. When Amy knocked, it swung open. That's all.

Amy led me into a room to the right of the front door. It was brightly lit—and filled with all sorts of cool stuff. A big-screen TV took up one wall. Next to it I saw a VCR, a five-CD player, a Sega *and* a Super Nintendo game system, and two speaker towers. Big leather couches circled a snack table that was piled high with chips, soda and cookies.

"Awesome!" I whispered to myself. The inside of this house was nothing like the outside.

Four or five girls in uniforms like Amy's knelt by the snack table, eating. Three others stood by the entertainment system. A couple more sat on the couch. One stood by the window.

I did a quick count in my head. Eleven girls. And Amy made twelve. Twelve new friends.

"Attention, everybody," Amy called. "This is Lizzy. She's our new recruit."

All eleven girls turned their heads at the exact same moment. "Hi, Lizzy," they called.

Amy walked me around the room, introducing me. There was a red-haired girl named Trudy, and a tall, thin girl named Violet. Priscilla had dark frizzy hair. Lorraine's was short and blond.

Pearl, a pretty girl with two long brown braids,

stood by the window. All the girls wore red sashes across their uniform, like Amy. All except Pearl. Hers was purple. Maybe that means she's some kind of troop leader, I guessed.

"Pearl, this is Lizzy," Amy said, introducing me. "She's from Waynesbridge."

Pearl smiled and stuck out her hand. "Cool. Welcome to my house, Lizzy. And welcome to the troop."

"Thanks," I replied, clasping her hand.

"Um, where's your scout leader?" I asked, gazing around the room, and back toward the front door.

"Oh, that would be Pearl's mother. She had to run some errands," Amy explained. "But she left us lots of snacks. Have some, Lizzy."

"Thanks," I said, eyeing the tortilla chips.

While I munched on some chips, Amy, Trudy, and Pearl took thick, green candles from a cupboard. They passed them out to the rest of the Camp Fear Girls, who lit them.

Then Trudy flicked out the ceiling light. Pearl moved to the front of our group.

"Didn't I promise you some scary fun?" Amy whispered, sitting next to me. "It's story time!"

I took a quick peek around the room. The green candles must have come from a special horror shop or something. Their light made everyone look spooky.

Cool, I thought. This was going to be great! Scary stories in a house on Fear Street!

I turned my attention back to Pearl, who was starting her story.

"Since Lizzy is new here, I will tell the story of the first troop of Camp Fear Girls." Pearl leaned forward and spoke in an eerie voice. "This story begins almost one hundred years ago. Thirteen girls—a troop of Shadyside scouts called the Camp Fear Girls—decided to go for a camp-out in the Fear Street Woods. Those thirteen girls left home and were never seen again."

"Their families searched and searched for these thirteen girls, but they were never found."

Pearl raised her candle to just below her chin.

"There are rumors—wild, horrible rumors," she continued, "that those thirteen scouts were turned into hideous monsters. By who—or what—no one knows."

As Pearl spoke, the candle cast strange shadows on the wall.

One shadow, behind Pearl, seemed larger than the others. I fixed my eyes on it. The shadow seemed to have a head. And sharp teeth. And claws!

A monster!

I blinked. The shadow was just a black blob again.

Wow! I was totally freaking myself out. Pearl's story was really creepy!

Pearl lowered her voice to a hoarse whisper. "Those monsters still roam Shadyside today, looking for new people to add to their troop.

"And once you join, you can never leave. You become one of the un-dead. Your body becomes like theirs. Your skin rots and falls off your bones. Your eyes sink back into your head. And you are forced to walk the earth that way—forever!"

My eyes went wide with horror.

I felt Amy tap me on the shoulder. "Pretty scary, huh, Lizzy?" she whispered in my ear.

I turned around to agree with her—and screamed!

Amy's skin was grayish-green.

One eye dangled—out of its socket.

A huge open cut ran down the side of her face. Green slime oozed from it.

Amy was a monster!

# About R. L. Stine

R. L. Stine, the creator of *Ghosts of Fear Street*, has written almost 100 scary novels for kids. The *Ghosts of Fear Street* series, like the *Fear Street* series, takes place in Shadyside and centers on the scary events that happen to people on Fear Street.

When he isn't writing, R. L. Stine likes to play pinball on his very own pinball machine, and explore New York City with his wife, Jane, and fifteen-year-old son, Matt.